CW01083106

Bello:
hidden talent rediscovered!

Bello is a digital only imprint of Pan Macmillan,
established to breathe new life into previously published,
classic books.

At Bello we believe in the timeless power of the imagination,
of good story, narrative and entertainment and we want to use
digital technology to ensure that many more readers
can enjoy these books into the future.

We publish in ebook and Print on Demand formats
to bring these wonderful books to new audiences.

About Bello:

www.panmacmillan.com/imprints/bello

About the author:

www.panmacmillan.com/author/francisdurbridge

Francis Durbridge

Francis Henry Durbridge was an English playwright and author born in Hull. In 1938, he created the character Paul Temple for the BBC radio serial *Send for Paul Temple*.

A crime novelist and detective, the gentlemanly Temple solved numerous crimes with the help of Steve Trent, a Fleet Street journalist who later became his wife. The character proved enormously popular and appeared in 16 radio serials and later spawned a 64-part big-budget television series (1969-71) and radio productions, as well as a number of comic strips, four feature films and various foreign radio productions.

Francis Durbridge also had a successful career as a writer for the stage and screen. His most successful play, *Suddenly at Home*, ran in London's West End for over a year.

Francis Durbridge

THE PASSENGER

First published in 1977 by Hodder and Stoughton

This edition published 2012 by Bello
an imprint of Pan Macmillan, a division of Macmillan Publishers Limited
Pan Macmillan, 20 New Wharf Road, London N1 9RR
Basingstoke and Oxford
Associated companies throughout the world

www.panmacmillan.com/imprints/bello
www.curtisbrown.co.uk

ISBN 978-1-4472-1509-7 EPUB
ISBN 978-1-4472-1508-0 POD

Visit www.panmacmillan.com to read more about all our books
and to buy them. You will also find features, author interviews and
news of any author events, and you can sign up for e-newsletters
so that you're always first to hear about our new releases.

Chapter One

David Walker stood staring out of the window, his hands in his pockets. He made himself breathe deeply and slowly as he struggled to get his anger and irritation under control. He'd been losing his temper too often and too easily lately, bursting out and saying things which he regretted as soon as he had spoken. Deep down inside himself he knew what the cause of it was, but he dared not bring it to the surface and face it. He had gone on pretending that things were still as they had always been between him and Evelyn, that the odd little signs he had noticed really meant nothing.

From up here in the office block he could look out over the whole area covered by the factory where Cavalier Toys were manufactured. It was one of the biggest toy factories in Europe and also an unusually attractive example of industrial architecture. The firm had moved from London when Guildfleet had been designated a development area and companies had been offered attractive inducements to establish premises there. After the cramped conditions in Hackney, the Trading Estate on the outskirts of the Buckinghamshire town seemed very spacious, allowing room for lawns and flowerbeds between the low buildings.

He lit a cigarette and turned to face the man who was sitting behind the large executive desk placed at an angle across one corner of the office.

"I'm sorry, Arthur. I didn't mean to lose my temper."

"For heaven's sake, David." Arthur Eastwood made a gesture with his hand as if to wave the apology away. "You're entitled to lose your temper once in a while."

"Once in a while is putting it mildly. I'm losing it far too often these days."

David Walker was ten years younger than his partner and was still two years on the right side of fifty. Though very different in a number of ways the two men had been a most effective team during the fifteen years since they had founded the firm in a small furniture factory whose owners had gone into liquidation. David was dark and still good-looking; he was careful about his appearance and bought his suits from a London tailor. Though unpredictable in his moods, it was he who produced the most original and novel ideas. Arthur Eastwood was more stolid and steady-going. He had a shrewd business mind and knew exactly how to put the brake on David's enthusiasm. His style of dressing suited his appearance, which had something of the country squire about it. He favoured tweeds and liked to make his suits last till the seats became shiny and his elbows began to wear thin.

Their most successful invention had been a toy known as The Walking Cavalier, an ingenious clockwork device representing a soldier of Charles I who could march with an extraordinarily life-like movement. In fact it had proved so successful that the firm had adopted the name Cavalier Toys. Various versions of the Cavalier adorned the Managing Director's office; a version in solid silver stood on Arthur Eastwood's desk.

David left the window and moved towards his partner's desk. "Well, where were we?"

"You were just about to tell me to take a running jump," Arthur said with a wry smile.

"Not you — Stenhouse."

"What have you got against Jack?" Arthur looked up, wrinkling his eyes against the afternoon sunshine which was pouring into the room.

"Nothing. I admire the little devil. He's a bomb. But I just don't want to finish up working for him."

"No one's asking you to." Arthur rose from his chair and came out from behind his desk. "You know the deal. They want to buy us out; the whole set up, lock, stock and barrel."

"Just like that." David snapped his fingers and threw a glance at the factory beyond the windows.

Arthur put a friendly hand on his shoulder. "Look, David, I know how you feel — but being sentimental about the firm won't get us anywhere."

David gave a short laugh. "After fifteen years I'm finding it a little difficult not to be sentimental."

"I know, but we've got to face up to things. Be realistic."

"And you think selling out to Jack Stenhouse is being realistic?"

"Yes, I do."

"In spite of the fact that last year we made more money than we've ever made before?"

"It's not just a question of money!" Arthur said with exasperation. "I'm fifty-seven, in two months' time I'll be fifty-eight."

"What's fifty-eight, for God's sake? Your old man didn't retire until he was seventy."

Arthur turned away and sat down in one of the easy chairs in front of his desk. "But he didn't have a coronary when he was fifty-five, David," he said quietly. There was an awkward pause before he asked: "Have you spoken to Evelyn about this?"

"Good heavens, no! You know Evelyn. She's not remotely interested in the business. She'd never even heard of Jack Stenhouse until I mentioned him at dinner the other night. And then she thought he was an actor."

Arthur gave a shrug. "She's not far wrong. Well — you know how I feel. It's up to you, David."

David stubbed out his half-smoked cigarette before replying. "When are we seeing Stenhouse again?"

"Tomorrow morning; ten o'clock."

"Here?" David's expression showed his surprise.

"Yes. And I've promised him a decision — one way or the other."

"He's certainly rushing things . . ."

"To be fair," Arthur pointed out, "this deal's been on the cards for almost two years now."

"It's a pity I didn't let you have your own way five years ago when you wanted to go public . . ."

Arthur laughed, but without bitterness. "Let's face it, David — you never have let me have my own way!"

"Perhaps it's time I started."

"Eh?" Arthur glanced up at him, obviously surprised.

David met his eye, his face serious and resigned. "We'll accept their offer. We'll give Stenhouse the go-ahead tomorrow morning."

"You mean that?" Arthur asked, trying not to show how relieved he was.

"Yes."

"You won't change your mind?"

"No, Arthur," David said, speaking with a seriousness which was unusual in him. "I won't change my mind."

Arthur nodded and reached for a cigar from the silver box on the front of his desk. He was piercing it preparatory to lighting up when the connecting door which led to David's office opened. Sue Denson came in warily. David's voice, raised in protest, had been audible through the walls.

David's secretary was in her late twenties and attractive in a slightly severe way. Her dark costume was in good taste, but subdued. Even a quick glance showed that she was a young woman who knew her own mind. She still wore her wedding ring on her left hand and, even though her marriage had broken up, liked to be called Mrs. Denson.

"Excuse me, Mr. Eastwood," she said to the older man. "I know I'm interrupting but Mr. Royce is on the telephone. He wants to speak to Mr. Walker."

"Tell him I'm out," David said curtly. "I'll 'phone him tomorrow morning. Oh — and ring Baker and cancel our appointment for this afternoon. I'm taking the rest of the day off, Sue."

Sue favoured him with a searching look, trying to guess the reason for such an uncharacteristic statement. "Aren't you feeling well, Mr. Walker?"

"I've got some shopping to do." David turned towards Arthur, who was now enveloped in a cloud of rich cigar smoke. "I've just discovered I've got to buy a shawl and a pair of slippers."

It was, in fact, almost unheard of for David Walker to 'take the rest of the day off'. One of the reasons for the firm's prosperity was that the partners were always in their offices before the workforce arrived and were still there after they left. It was a rule that one or other of them would go round the works at least once a day and talk to the men. As a result there had never been a strike at Cavalier Toys. Such results are not achieved without effort, but in his present mood David could not help feeling that it had all been wasted effort. What was the point of dedicating most of your waking hours to building up something and when you've achieved your aim just handing it over lock, stock and barrel to a complete outsider?

The friendly greetings of the employees he met on his way to the car park only made him feel worse. He knew them all by name. How would they feel when they heard the news?

He opened the door of the Bentley and slid behind the wheel. The security man on the gate raised the bar as the big car swung towards the exit, and raised a hand in salute as David turned out onto the road. But instead of heading towards the town centre he took the road leading to the residential district where his own house was. He just hoped that Evelyn would be at home. He had to unburden his feelings onto someone and she was really the only person who would understand how deeply he felt. She knew all too well how many evenings and weekends he had sacrific-xl in the interests of the firm.

The drive only took five minutes. The big engine turned so effortlessly that it was practically inaudible as he turned in at the gate of Gameswood House. It was a solid brick building, built in the thirties, with enough trees in its grounds to shield it from the houses flanking it on either side.

The avenue was short. David at once spotted the car which was parked outside his front door. It was an Austin Allegro with 'L' plates bearing the emblem 'Norton School of Motoring'. David smiled as he stopped his car behind it. Evelyn had been trying for so long to pass her driving test that it had become a joke between them.

The Bentley's door closed with the dignified coach-built click which always gave him satisfaction. He was feeling in his pocket for his keys as he went up the steps to the front door. He was still smiling, thinking up some remark to tease Evelyn about the bill she was running up for driving lessons.

He closed the door and as he turned his glance fell on the hall table. A man's hat and a pair of leather driving-gloves had been placed on it. Assuming Evelyn and her instructor must be in the drawing-room — probably swotting up the Highway Code — he made for the door of the big front room. Before he reached it he heard a murmur of voices from upstairs. He checked, moved to the bottom of the staircase and was about to call up when the sound of a woman's laugh froze him. It had to be Evelyn, but there was something odd about that laugh, at the same time girlish and sensual.

A door had opened on the corridor above. He heard her say: "You'll have to be patient, Roy. I'll be back in a sec."

From the room beyond came the murmur of a man's voice, the words indistinguishable. Then she came into view, still laughing as she looked over her shoulder at the bedroom doorway.

"Don't be silly, sweetie. You'll just have to wait."

She was wearing a flimsy organza dressing-gown, transparent enough for him to see the curves of her naked body underneath it. She had tied the waist-belt hastily round her middle. Her golden hair was tousled and the lipstick round her mouth was smeared. But it was the strange excitement in her eyes which shook him most. They were alight with a fire which he had not seen for years.

She had started to come down the stairs before she saw him. She stopped dead and then, with startling suddenness, all expression drained from her face. David shook his head, as if to clear it of a nightmare. For five terrible seconds they just stared at each other, while the whole of their life together crumbled silently round them.

Then David turned away, his face twisting with grief and revulsion. He blundered towards the door, clumsily let himself out and disappeared.

Arthur Eastwood went on listening to the ringing tone at the other end of the line long after he knew that there was going to be no reply. From across the office Jack Stenhouse was watching him impatiently, a frown on his confident, arrogant features. He was in his mid-forties and already going bald on top. As if to compensate, he had allowed his side-whiskers to grow well out onto his cheeks. They added to his tough, almost predatory appearance.

"Still no reply." Arthur replaced the receiver at last and pressed a button on his desk. "I'm terribly sorry about this, Jack. It's most unlike David. Most mornings he's in his office well before I am. We have a sort of running joke about it."

"It must be wearing a little thin." Stenhouse looked pointedly at his watch. "I'm sorry, Arthur — I'll have to be making a move."

"Yes, of course. You're a very busy man these days, I realise that." Arthur stood up as Stenhouse picked up his coat and hat from one of the upright chairs.

"It's a pity your partner doesn't."

The door from David's office had opened to admit a worried-looking Sue Denson. "Any news, Sue?" Arthur asked her.

"No, I'm afraid not."

Something about her hesitant manner made Arthur glance sharply at her. "Have you spoken to Despatch?"

"Yes. They haven't seen Walker since yesterday morning."

"All right, Sue. Keep ringing his home — there's bound to be a reply sooner or later."

Sue nodded. She seemed thankful to escape back into David's office. Arthur helped Stenhouse into his coat, an expensive affair with a fur collar and scarlet silk lining.

"There's nothing to worry about, Jack. He's made his mind up, and once David . . ."

"*I'm* not worried, my dear fellow, not in the slightest," Stenhouse said, somehow making the reassurance sound like a threat.

"I'll get David to give you a ring, the moment he comes in."

"Yes, do that. I'm leaving for New York on Saturday morning. If I haven't heard from him by Thursday morning you can forget the whole thing." Stenhouse's manner had become distant as he offered his hand.

Arthur put a hand on his arm in an attempt at a friendly gesture. "I'll come down to the car with you."

The door had scarcely closed behind them when David walked through from his own office. His face was haggard and depressed. It was obvious that he had not shaved and his usually immaculate suit looked as if he had slept in it. He was followed by a deeply concerned Sue.

"Thank you, Sue. I just couldn't have faced them."

"Can I get you anything, Mr. Walker?"

"No, no, I don't want anything at the moment."

"Janet's making some coffee," Sue said, in the voice of a mother coaxing a reluctant child. "Let me get you a cup . . ."

David rubbed his hands over his eyes. "All right, Sue, I'll have some coffee. And get me a call to Ditchford. A personal call to a Mr. Parker, Ditchford 278."

"Ditchford 278."

"Yes. It's in Cumberland, near Penrith."

Sue hesitated, as if she was about to say something, then tightened her lips and returned to her office.

David walked listlessly over to the window. Looking down he saw Arthur and Jack Stenhouse emerge from the building and move towards the car park. Stenhouse was striding ahead, Arthur almost having to run to keep up with him. In the car park the door of a mauve Rolls-Royce Corniche opened and a uniformed chauffeur stepped out. He was holding the door of the rear compartment as Stenhouse arrived. Arthur was still talking as the burly man climbed into his car. He put out a hand and slammed the door, cutting Arthur's sentence off before he had completed it. Arthur was left standing dejectedly as the big saloon glided away. As he turned back towards the office block he suddenly saw David's unmistakable green Bentley. He glanced up towards the window and began to hurry back.

When Arthur burst into his office David was standing beside the desk, the telephone in his hand. Eastwood stamped to the window, fuming.

"I'm not sure what time I'll arrive," David was saying, "probably about five o'clock. No, I'm driving up . . . What? I'll tell you when I see you, Uncle."

Arthur had hardly been able to contain his annoyance. As the receiver was replaced he rounded on his partner. "David, where the hell have you been? Stenhouse waited almost an hour!"

"I know . . . I'm sorry, Arthur."

David's voice had been very tense. Arthur stared at him, noting the unshaven face, the crumpled clothes. "What the devil happened?"

"I — I just couldn't face Jack Stenhouse — not this morning."

"Have you changed your mind?"

"Ehmm?" David had hardly heard the question. His thoughts were far away.

"About the deal?" Arthur said impatiently.

"No, no." David's voice was still vague. "I haven't changed my mind."

Arthur moved towards him, his anger changing to concern. "David, what the hell's happened?"

Abruptly David sat down and put his head in his hands. Arthur waited and after a moment he looked up again. "Do you know a man called Roy Norton?"

"Yes. He runs a driving school. Tallish chap, good-looking." "That's him. Well, I met the gentleman — somewhat unexpectedly, I'm afraid — yesterday afternoon."

"Well?" Arthur asked, still not getting the drift of David's remarks.

"Evelyn introduced us," David said in a flat, unemotional voice.

"Evelyn . . .?"

"Yes."

"Yesterday afternoon?"

"That's right."

Only then did Arthur realise what his partner was trying to tell him. "Oh, my God," he said softly. "David, I'm sorry."

"But not surprised?" Arthur glanced away, dodging the question.

9

"Not surprised, Arthur? The little bitch! The mean, cheap, despicable little bitch! I could have killed her!"

David's voice had risen to near hysteria. Arthur did not like to see a man lose control of himself. He turned towards the window as David once again buried his head in his hands.

"What happened?"

"There were so many things I wanted to say to both of them, but . . ."

"What happened, David?" Arthur insisted quietly.

"I — I didn't say a word. Not a bloody word. I . . . I just walked out . . ."

In the silence they could hear Sue's typewriter clattering in the adjacent office.

"What are you going to do?"

"I don't know. I suppose ultimately I'll have to think about a divorce or . . . Anyway, I'm going away for two or three days. I've got an uncle in Cumberland. He looked after me when I was a boy and I haven't seen him for years. I thought I'd stay with him."

"I think that's a good idea."

David pushed himself to his feet and went to the cabinet where samples of Cavalier Toys were displayed.

"It's come at an awkward time for you, Arthur, I realise that. But I've got to get away." He went to stand behind his partner's shoulder. "I'm sorry about this morning."

"This morning?"

"Stenhouse."

"Oh, to hell with Jack!" Arthur exclaimed, dragging his eyes from the articulated lorry which was just reversing into one of the loading bays.

"I'll 'phone him later. I'll straighten it out."

"If you'd like to move in with us for a little while, you're very welcome. You know that."

Arthur put a hand round his partner's shoulder and shepherded him back towards the group of easy chairs.

"Thanks, Arthur." David spoke with a kind of vague gratitude. "Can I talk about it when I get back?"

The weather at least was kind to David for his drive to the North He set off in good time knowing that he had the whole day to get to Cumberland. He had no intention of travelling by the featureless motorway. He preferred to travel by a route of his own, which took him through attractive towns and pleasant scenery. For the first time since that ghastly moment at the foot of his own staircase he felt a kind of peace. Driving the Bentley always had a soothing effect on him. It was reassuring to see the long bonnet stretching out ahead of him, to know that he had immense reserves of power there, ready to obey his vall if he needed them.

For the moment he was ambling along minor roads, following a route that would take him northwards somewhere between the M1 and the A1. The sun was sparkling on the green cellulose and chromium radiator and the fields on either side of the road were green and fresh.

The blue Ford Capri had been on his tail for some time now. He had been watching it in his mirror, wondering if the driver was too hesitant to pass the big saloon. He slowed slightly, lowered the window and waved it on. The Ford went past with a rush of acceleration and had soon disappeared round a bend ahead.

A few miles further on he slowed to a halt in order to cross a major road. Diagonally opposite him was an attractive hotel with a huge wistaria clambering up its walls. He could already see the girl standing at the roadside opposite it. She had picked up her small bag and was watching him expectantly and he had no doubt that she was going to try and thumb a lift. As soon as the road was clear he accelerated across. The girl came right out into the roadway, disdaining the usual hitch-hiker's thumbing gesture and positively waving at him to stop.

She was an extremely pretty girl in her early twenties, wearing a set of fairly new jeans and with a cheeky cap on the side of her head. David glanced at her as he went past. He made it a rule not to give lifts to stray young women, but there was something innocent and appealing about this girl. Her face fell as she saw that he intended to ignore her signals and as he gathered speed he was left with the impression of an almost despairing disappointment.

He relented almost at once. Perhaps she had been waiting there for hours and, after all, there was plenty of room in the Bentley. He found himself applying the brake before he had time to really analyse his feelings. In the mirror he could see her running up the roadside after him, hefting the bag which contained her gear. He opened the door as she came level with the car. She arrived, gasping and smiling, threw her bag onto the back and scrambled into the passenger's seat. He leaned across to close the door himself before she could slam it.

"Ah, that's nice."

She snuggled down in the leather seat and looked round the car with satisfaction as he moved off again. David was slightly amused by her calm assumption that she had a natural right to ride free in somebody else's car. She had not even bothered to say thanks. As the car regained its normal cruising speed, he could see out of the corner of his eye that she was studying his profile.

"How far are you going?" she asked suddenly.

"Er — Penrith." Caution and a certain suspicion of unaccompanied young women made David reluctant to disclose his exact destination.

"Penrith? Where's that?"

"Cumberland. Not far from Appleby."

"Appleby? Never heard of it! Anyway, do you go through Doncaster?"

"Yes."

"Well that's okay," she said, nodding. "You can drop me in Doncaster."

"Any particular street?"

She looked at him with a smile but seemed quite unaware of the sarcasm in his voice.

"No, anywhere will do." She squirmed round to sit sideways in the seat, noting all the special fittings in the Mulliner saloon. "Nice car. Very posh."

"I'm glad you like it," David said, still with the same ironic tone.

"You must have pots of money."

He laughed. "Yes, I'm very rich."

She shot him a quick glance, still not sure whether to take him seriously or not. "What are you going to Appleby for?"

"Penrith."

"I mean Penrith."

"I'm thinking of buying it."

"Buying it! The whole place?"

"Yes. It's very small."

She slid down in her seat, frowning and pouting slightly. "You're pulling my leg, aren't you?'

"Yes, I'm pulling your leg."

For the first time he looked at her properly. She grinned back at him and suddenly he was glad that he had broken his rule. There was something out of the ordinary about this girl.

"It makes a nice change," she said with a laugh. "It's usually dirty stories."

David smiled and transferred his attention to the road again. She did not try to open the conversation till they had passed through a village.

"Do you smoke?" she asked him suddenly.

At first he thought she was offering him a cigarette. Then he realised from the expectant look on her face that this was her way of asking him for one. He withdrew his case from his pocket and handed it to her.

"Thanks." She took a cigarette and put it between her lips, closed the case and then examined it with interest. "D.W . . . What's that stand for?"

"Those are my initials."

"I know that! I'm not that stupid! D — let's see now. Derek?" She put her head on one side to size him up. "No, I don't think so . . . Donald? No, you don't look like a Donald to me. Denis, perhaps?" As David made no reply she nodded positively. "Yes, Denis."

"David." David was smiling. She had somehow managed to make the simple guessing game charming and amusing.

"Oh — oh, I like David!" she exclaimed enthusiastically. "I used to know a David. Knew him well, as a matter of fact." She paused, as if to let the significance of this remark sink in. "My name's Judy."

David gave her an amused glance, but he did not pick up the cue. Instead he put his hand out for his cigarette case and restored it to his pocket. He pressed the cigar lighter fitted into the dashboard, waited a few seconds, then held the glowing red element for her as she lit her cigarette. She nodded thanks and drew smoke deep into her lungs.

"Do you mind if I switch the radio on?"

"No," David said, amused by her possessive and confident manner and wondering why he did not find it annoying.

She leaned forward and began to spin the tuning knob, searching for a suitable programme.

The music was not what David himself would have chosen but at least it kept her occupied. He did not like to talk when he was driving and she seemed quite happy to chatter away without expecting any reply from him. Most of her remarks consisted of a running commentary, usually scathing, of the records being played by the disc jockey.

They had travelled several miles when he realised she had asked him a question and was waiting for an answer.

"What did you say?"

"Do you and your wife always take separate holidays?"

"This isn't a holiday," he replied curtly. "And what makes you think I'm married?"

"Aren't you?"

"Yes, I am, as a matter of fact. Technically, at any rate. Look, why don't you put the seat back and have a nap?"

"I'm not sleepy. Besides, I'm very fussy who I sleep with." Her mischievous smile flashed again as she saw his frown of annoyance. "Now *I'm* pulling *your* leg."

David did not return the smile. He nodded towards the glove pocket. "There's a magazine in that pocket if you'd like to look at it."

"Is that a polite way of telling me to shut up?" Judy asked, still good-humoured. She finally found the lipstick for which she had been rummaging in her handbag and took the top off.

"Yes."

"I thought it was!" She pushed her lips forward as she prepared to overhaul her make-up. "You sound just like . . . Oh, hell!"

"What is it?"

"My lipstick! I think it's fallen under the seat." She leaned forward and began to grope about under the seat. "I can't feel it."

"Don't worry." David's voice was really irritated now. The chatter and antics of his companion were beginning to lose some of their charm. "We'll find it when you get out of the car."

He had hardly spoken when the engine faltered. It coughed and then picked up again, only to die a few seconds later. David ran the car onto the verge of the road as it coasted to a halt.

"What's the matter?"

"I don't know, it seems as if . . ." David ran his eye over the dials on the dashboard. "Oh damn! Blast!"

"What is it?"

"I've run out of petrol!" He switched the ignition off. "The tank's empty."

"You nut!" Judy was laughing at him now. "You're not really with it today, are you, Buster?"

"Blast!" David glared at her with real annoyance. This was the consequence of picking up people who took your mind off your driving. "Didn't we pass a garage a couple of miles back?"

"Yes, I think we did. On the left-hand side. Why? What are you going to do?"

"What the hell do you think I'm going to do!" David almost shouted. "I'm going to get some petrol!"

He got out of the car and opened the boot. There was a petrol can in there, but he knew that he had emptied it when he had filled up the lawn mower. As he was about to move away she wound down the window and poked her head out.

"Where's that magazine?"

"I told you! In the side pocket."

He rurned his back on her and began to trudge along the road in the direction from which he had come.

It was a good half hour before the garage's breakdown Land-Rover drew up behind the Bentley. David climbed out, holding the refilled two-gallon can in his hand. He reached in his pocket, found a 50p piece and handed it to the driver.

"Thanks, guy. You'll be okay now?"

"Yes. Thanks for your help."

"You're welcome."

The Land-Rover turned in the road, its driver working energetically at the steering wheel. He waved cheerfully as he drove away towards the garage.

David moved to the rear of the Bentley, removed the filler cap of the petrol tank and was about to pour the two gallons of petrol in when he noticed that the passenger's seat was unoccupied. He put the can down and went round to the window on that side. The car was empty. A page had been torn from the copy of 'Drive' which he'd been carrying in the glove compartment. It had been folded in two and hung across the steering wheel. He reached across and opened it out. A lipstick had been used to scrawl the message in bold capital letters.

BYE, THANKS FOR THE LIFT. J.

The magazine from which the page had been torn lay on the seat. Presumably she had grown tired of waiting and had used her very individual hitch-hiking methods to persuade some other driver to take her on. The girl had been rather maddening, but it was with a peculiar sense of loneliness and loss that David stared up the road ahead. Then he shrugged the mood off, crumpled the message and threw it into the hedge. He went to the back of the car, emptied the can into the tank and went round to see if the car would start. She fired straight away. He closed his door and drove on.

About a week or five days after his partner had departed for his holiday in the North of England, Arthur Eastwood was seated in his office dictating letters into the machine mounted on the special drawer fitted to the side of his desk. He heard the door of David Walker's office but, thinking it was Sue Denson, did not look up.

He frowned and raised his voice, endeavouring to preserve his concentration till he had concluded the letter.

" . . .with all due respect, it would appear to us that you are deliberately confusing the issue. Only last Monday . . ."

He broke off as he became aware that the person who had come in was not Sue but David Walker himself. He quickly put the microphone down and stood up.

"David! I had no idea you were back!"

"I got back last night," David told him calmly.

Arthur came round his desk, his eyes searching his partner's face. David looked less haggard than when he had last seen him, but something fundamental in him had changed and his face was already thinner.

"My dear fellow, you should have 'phoned me! How are you? I didn't expect to see you for at least another three or four days."

David shrugged, as if the matter of his health was of minor importance. "I'm all right, but — going away wasn't such a good idea after all, I'm afraid."

Arthur hesitated, as if trying to decide whether to reopen a painful subject, then made his mind up. He said quietly: "I saw Evelyn on Tuesday. . . ."

David's eyes immediately jerked towards him. "Where?"

"In the High Street."

"What happened?"

"I don't think she saw me." Arthur scratched his cheek wryly. "If she did she made a pretty good job of looking the other way."

"Was she alone?" David asked after a moment.

"Yes. You haven't seen her, I take it?"

"No, I didn't go back to the house last night. I was tired and depressed and just didn't feel like having a row with anyone."

Arthur noticed a new stoop in David's shoulders as he went and stood looking gloomily out of the window.

"Where did you stay?"

"I've taken a room at The Crown; for the time being at any rate."

"You should have stayed with us, you know. I imagine you'll

have to go back to the house sooner or later, if only to collect your things."

"Yes, I suppose I will." David turned round, squaring his shoulders as if determined to shake off the depression of the past week. "Well — what's been happening here? How's the Stenhouse situation?"

"You might well ask!" Arthur gave a short laugh. "I'm getting fifteen telephone calls a day."

"From Jack?"

"No, he's in New York. From the accountants. And letters!" Arthur gestured towards the pile of correspondence on his IN tray. "Just take a look at that lot!"

Down in the visitors' car park a CID car from Guildfleet police station had just stopped with its bonnet a few inches from the low parapet which defined the parking area. Both the officers who stepped out were wearing light overcoats and hats, and in their civilian clothes carried no badges to indicate their rank. Yet even to a casual observer it was evident that Detective-Inspector Martin Denson was the senior. Though still in his early thirties, an air of authority showed in his tough, determined and unsmiling features. He was a big man, a shade over six foot, but quick and purposeful in his movements. He was light on his feet and Detective-Sergeant Kennedy had to step out to keep abreast of him as they moved towards the entrance to the office block.

They were just running up the steps to the double swing-doors when Sue Denson came out, a sheaf of papers in her hand. Seeing her, Sergeant Kennedy dropped back, his face instinctively adopting the policeman's expressionless mask.

"Good morning, Sue," Martin said gravely.

Sue Denson ignored the greeting of her husband. She looked straight past him at the Detective-Sergeant.

"Hello, Harry!" she said with forced friendliness. "How's Dorothy?"

Embarrassed though he was, Kennedy tried to smile. "Oh, she's . . . fine, thank you, Sue."

"And the children?"

"Yes — yes, they're great."

"How are you, Sue?" Martin broke in, still in his quiet, serious voice. Kennedy thought he sounded as if he really cared, but the brief glance which Sue gave him was cold and remote.

"Martin, I'm extremely busy this morning. What is it you want?"

"Tell your boss I'd like to see him." Martin's voice had abruptly changed. This was the police officer speaking.

"My boss?" Sue blinked, shaken by the sudden edge in Martin's tone.

"You do work for a Mr. David Walker?"

"You know I do," she said, with something like her old spirit.

"Then kindly tell him I want to see him."

Sue noticed for the first time the official-looking briefcase in Kennedy's hand. She looked from one face to the other and was met with uncompromising, businesslike stares. Clutching the sheaf of papers more closely to her, she turned and led the way into the building.

As she entered the office to tell her employer that the Inspector and Sergeant were waiting to see him, Arthur Eastwood was again on the telephone, and to judge by his voice the person on the other end was being extremely irritating.

" . . .yes, but that's not the point, it was despatched on the 18th . . . Forgive me, but just for once I do happen to know what I'm talking about! All right, you do that . . . No, you go ahead and do that!"

He slammed the receiver down and wiped his brow.

"Excuse me, Mr. Eastwood," Sue said, and then turned with some embarrassment towards David. "My hus . . . There's an Inspector Denson to see you."

David was standing beside Arthur's desk. He had been going through the pile of letters awaiting attention.

"Oh?" he said, raising an enquiring eyebrow at Arthur. "Well, you'd better show him in, Sue."

As the door closed David came round to the front of the desk. "Denson? Is this the chap she's married to?"

"I imagine so. He's in the Force."

"Have you met him?"

"Once. We played in a golf tournament about a year ago, shortly after she walked out on him. He never spoke a word — just knocked hell out of me."

Arthur was laughing at the memory when Sue opened the door to admit the two officers. Arthur went to meet the Inspector with outstretched hand.

"Hello, Mr. Denson! Come in!"

"Good morning, Mr. Eastwood." Martin shook hands in his characteristically non-committal way.

"Nice to see you again," Arthur said warmly, and could not resist adding: "How's the golf?"

Martin permitted himself a faint smile. "It's non-existent at the moment, I'm afraid."

Arthur nodded at Martin and looked at David with a wry twinkle in his eye. "This chap's the longest hitter I've ever seen. You remember the old fourteenth at St. George's? I've seen him on the green in one . . ."

"I'm sorry to disturb you, Mr. Walker." Martin's brisk tone curtly interrupted Arthur's reminiscence. "But I wonder if you could spare me a few minutes?"

"Yes, of course," David said, surprised at the seriousness of the Inspector's tone.

Martin gestured towards his companion. "This is a colleague of mine, Sergeant Kennedy."

"Good morning, sir." Kennedy nodded, his eye meeting David's appraisingly.

"Good morning."

"If this is a private matter . . ." Arthur Eastwood said, his expression suggesting that his presence might be embarrassing for David.

"This is your office, Arthur!" David told him firmly. "Sit down."

Arthur obediently went behind his desk and resumed his seat. David motioned the two detectives towards chairs and sat down himself.

"What is it you want to see me about?"

The Sergeant had placed his briefcase on his knees and was undoing the zip.

Martin came directly to the point. "Do you know a girl called Judy Clayton, sir?"

"No, I'm afraid I don't," David said without hesitation.

"She lives in Guildfleet; she has a bed-sitter in Reigate Street."

"I've never heard of her."

Martin's answer was to nod at Kennedy. Kennedy withdrew a photograph from the brief-case and handed it to David. David tried in vain to read Martin's expression before he took the photograph. He studied it for a moment and Arthur saw a curious shadow pass across his face.

David looked up into Martin's searching eyes. "Is this Judy Clayton?"

"Yes, it is."

"Then I'm sorry," David said quietly. "I do know the girl. I gave her a lift in my car."

"When was that, sir?"

"Last Tuesday. I was driving up North to see an uncle of mine and I .. Look, what is this? Has something happened to this girl?"

Martin ignored David's question, and persisted with his own interrogation. "Where did you pick up Miss Clayton, sir?"

"About — ten miles the other side of Guildfleet. She was standing on a corner trying to thumb a lift."

"Tell me what happened."

David's face showed the irritation he was feeling at Martin's dogged questions. "What do you mean? Nothing happened. She said she was going to Doncaster and I simply offered her a lift."

"Did you take her as far as Doncaster, sir?"

"No, I didn't."

"Why not?"

"Because I . . ." David glanced across at Arthur, bewildered by the hint of menace underlying this string of questions. Arthur's face was grave as if he had already guessed where all this was leading. He gave David a slight nod as if prompting him to co-operate and answer the Inspector's questions. "She'd been in the car about half an hour when I ran out of petrol. Fortunately, we'd just passed a garage — well, about two miles back. I walked to that garage and one of the mechanics drove me back to the car."

"And what about the girl? Did she go to the garage with you?"

"No, of course not!" David told him angrily. "She sat in the car and read a magazine."

"Go on, Mr. Walker," Martin prompted, completely unmoved by David's unfriendly response.

"Well — that's it. When I got back she'd gone."

"Gone where, sir?"

"How do I know?" David said belligerently. "I imagine she got tired of waiting and finally persuaded someone else to pick her up. There was a note on the driving wheel thanking me for the lift."

"Look, what the devil's this all about, Inspector?" Arthur cut in, his curiosity getting the better of him. "Is this girl missing or something?"

"She's not missing, sir. She's dead. She was strangled. We found her body about three hundred yards from where Mr. Walker's car stopped. Or perhaps I should say — three hundred yards from where we found this."

Martin reached into his breast pocket and brought out a plain white envelope from which he carefully extracted a sheet of printed paper. Even as he unfolded the crumpled sheet, David recognised it as the page of 'Drive' on which Judy had scrawled her lipstick message.

"I rather imagine this is the note you were referring to, sir?"

"Yes. Yes, it is." David gave a nervous laugh and immediately wished he hadn't. "I was just beginning to curse myself for having thrown it away."

"One would hardly have expected you to have kept it, Mr. Walker." Martin carefully refolded the page, replaced it in the envelope and returned it to his pocket.

"Inspector," Arthur said, "how did you know it was David's car that picked up this girl? His name isn't on the note."

"We made enquiries in the district and the garage-hand remembered both the Bentley and Mr. Walker. He gave us a very good description of you, sir. We also found this in the girl's handbag."

This time it was a key-ring which Martin extracted from his pocket. He held it up between his index finger and thumb. The key-ring was one of the clasp variety. On it were three small keys and a metal emblem.

"That's one of our key-rings!" Arthur was leaning forward, staring at the reproduction of his company's most successful product — the Walking Cavalier. "The firm's I mean . . ."

"Yes, sir. I imagine you give them away to customers." Martin switched his gaze meaningly from Arthur to David. "And friends."

"Well, that's the idea. It's an advertisement."

"Did you give this to Miss Clayton, sir?" Martin asked, still looking at David.

"Of course I didn't! Why on earth should I give a complete stranger . . ." David broke off, struck by a sudden thought.

"Go on, sir."

"I didn't give it to her, but now I come to think about it, I've a pretty shrewd idea where she got it from. It's my bet she took it out of the glove pocket of my car."

"Was there a key-ring like this in the glove pocket?"

"There's at least half a dozen of them."

"We always carry them around with us, Inspector," Arthur explained. "I've got a stack of 'em at home."

"Well, if what you say is true," Martin pointed out, "she certainly didn't waste any time putting her keys on it. It's curious we didn't find her old one."

"Her old one?"

"Her old key-ring."

"Look, Inspector." David's voice rose as his anger returned. "What are you inferring? That I knew the girl? That she was a friend of mine? That I gave her the key-ring long before . . ."

"I wasn't aware that I was inferring anything, sir," Martin said, his eyes innocent. "But since you raise the point — was she a friend of yours?"

"No! I've told you, I'd never seen her before!"

"She was standing on the corner and you just offered her a lift?"

"Yes."

"Did she tell you why she was standing on that particular corner, sir?"

"No, she didn't."

Martin paused before playing his trump card.

"She had an appointment to meet someone there," he said, watching David carefully. "At ten-thirty."

"Ten-thirty?" David echoed, his forehead puckering. "Yes."

"But — it must have been about ten-thirty when I picked her up."

"Yes, I suppose it must have been, sir," Martin said, his voice almost soothing.

David ran his tongue over his lips and exchanged a worried glance with Arthur.

"How do you know she had this appointment, Inspector?" Arthur asked, after a few moments silence.

"We found a diary in her handbag. It mentioned the appointment but unfortunately it didn't mention who it was with." Martin stood up. Kennedy zipped up his briefcase and followed suit. The Inspector offered David his hand. His manner was as friendly as if he was completely satisfied with David's answers. "Well, thank you, sir. You've given me the information I wanted. We won't take up any more of your time."

"I take it you're in the book, sir," Kennedy said casually, "if we want to get in touch with you?"

"What? Oh, yes . . . No, I'm sorry — just at the moment I'm staying at The Crown."

Kennedy, who had been moving towards the door, checked in obvious surprise. "In Mortimer Street?"

"Yes." David met his enquiring gaze defiantly, as if daring him to start up a whole new line of interrogation. But Kennedy simply exchanged a look with his superior and nodded.

"Thank you, sir."

Arthur had hurried round from behind his desk. He was on the

Inspector's heels as he went out through the door. "I'll come with you, Inspector," he said, throwing David a look which told him as plainly as words to stay where he was.

Arthur had seen that David's reaction to the police enquiries had made a very unfavourable impression on the Inspector. It had really been most unfortunate that the officers had turned up at a moment when David was off balance. Although Arthur knew exactly why his partner had been so edgy and resentful there was, of course, no reason for the detectives to be aware of the true cause of his brusque and unhelpful manner. As they went along the corridor and descended the stairs to the entrance foyer, he gave Martin a low-voiced account of the shock David had received when he had gone back to Gameswood House that afternoon nearly a week ago.

Martin listened carefully, merely nodding from time to time. Arthur was silent as they crossed the carpeted foyer. The girl at the reception desk was watching them curiously and he did not want her to overhear what he was saying.

Outside the doors Martin put on his hat and offered Arthur his hand.

"Thank you, Mr. Eastwood, I'm grateful to you for putting me in the picture."

"I just didn't want you to get the wrong impression. My partner's not usually bad-tempered, I assure you. But this business with his wife, well — it's knocked the poor devil sideways."

"I rather imagine it has, sir." He searched his memory for a moment. "Roy Norton? Doesn't he run a driving school?"

"Yes, that's the chap."

Martin nodded. "I know the man. Thank you again, sir. You've been most helpful."

Arthur slipped in through the swing-doors and the two CID men went down the steps. As they moved towards the car park Martin cast an almost envious look at David's Bentley, parked with its dignified bonnet facing a reserved space marked 'Mr. David Walker'.

"Do you think he was telling the truth, Harry?"

"Walker? Yes, I believe him, but whether I would have done if the girl hadn't left that note . . . I don't know."

"You attach importance to the note?"

"Don't you?" Kennedy asked, surprised.

Martin paused with one hand on the door of the police car, staring back at the Bentley.

"A great deal of importance. Especially since she may not have written it."

"May not have written it? What do you mean?"

"The note was written in lipstick; in block capitals," Martin reminded him. "According to the lab the lipstick's known as Pink Flamingo. That's the name the makers give it."

"Well?"

"The lipstick we found in her handbag was called Mountain Rose."

"Mountain Rose? You mean it was a different shade?" "That's right."

"Well — which one was she wearing?"

"That's the interesting point," Martin said, opening the door and stooping to enter the car. "She wasn't wearing any lipstick."

Martin Denson had found it unbearable to continue living in the cottage after he and Sue had broken up. It was a charming place just outside Guildfleet, but every detail of the house and garden reminded him of Sue and the happy years they had spent together before suddenly and inexplicably things had gone wrong. Luckily a small bachelor flat just off the High Street had come up for sale and the bank had granted him a bridging loan to tide him over until the estate agents found a buyer for the cottage. He had moved in as much furniture as he needed, but there just was not room in the flat for the contents of the cottage. He hoped to make some deal with the new purchaser to take over what was left there.

The flat still had the look of being temporarily occupied. Most of the furniture was more or less where the removal men had put it. Frankly, Martin did not care about the aesthetic effect of his quarters. It was just a place to eat and sleep in. He could never look upon it as a home. In fact, he knew that he could never look on anywhere as home unless Sue was there too. The place had the advantage that it was only a few minutes' walk from the police station and, since Martin had sought consolation and forgetfulness by immersing himself totally in his work, he did not object to being so readily on call.

He had long ago given up keeping the place tidy. Books and long-playing records were scattered over the chairs and tables. Martin had brought with him the two features in his personal life which he could still enjoy in solitude — his Dynatron Hi-Fi system and his personal library of books.

The morning after the visit to the Cavalier Toys factory he was just coming out of the small kitchen with a heaped plate of cereals in his hand when the front door bell sounded. He put the plate down and went through to open the door. Harry Kennedy was standing on the mat outside. He had a briefcase in his hand and there was an expression of excitement on his youthful, suntanned face.

"Hello, Harry!" Martin greeted him, in some surprise.

"Am I disturbing you?"

"Yes," Martin replied, with that straight-faced expression which made it so hard to tell when he was serious and when he was pulling your leg.

"I'm sorry, Inspector, but it's important."

Martin had to smile at Kennedy's suddenly worried expression. He held the door open wide. "Come in!"

"I tried to get hold of you last night," Kennedy said, as he walked through the hall into the sitting-room, "but there was no reply."

"It was my mother's birthday; I went over to Hampstead." Martin gestured towards the table where books and magazines had been pushed back to make room for his breakfast tray. "Coffee?"

"No, thanks."

Martin shrugged and sat down at the table. He picked up the spoon and pulled the plate of cereals towards him. "Well — what's happened? You're steamed up about something . . ."

Kennedy sat down on the edge of one of the easy-chairs and began to unzip his bulging briefcase. "I went back to Reigate Street last night — Judy Clayton's place."

"Yes?" Martin prompted, munching Rice Crispies.

"Mrs. Bodley — the landlady — finally produced the key."

"Don't tell me Mrs. Bodley's beginning to co-operate!"

"No, she still won't talk; she shuts up like a clam when the murder's mentioned." Kennedy withdrew an envelope and a bulky object from the briefcase. He was looking decidedly pleased with himself. "However, I discovered this interesting little item in the cupboard, amongst the various odds and ends."

Martin put his spoon down and watched with interest as Kennedy unfastened the leather case and took out a square folded camera. He handed it to Martin, who accepted it with an enquiring lift of the eyebrows.

"It's one of those new Polaroids — what do you call 'em? They take instant pictures, you don't have to . . ." He stared unseeing at the litter of books on the sofa, then snapped his fingers as he remembered. "SX-70!" He examined the camera for a moment, and pressed a red knob. The camera clicked open. "Yes — and it's a very good one, too."

Kennedy shook half a dozen prints out of the envelope and stood up to lay them on the table in front of the Inspector. "These are some of the pictures she took. I found them with the camera."

Martin pushed his plate aside and leaned his elbows on the table to study the little collection. They had all obviously been taken at some holiday resort, probably on the Mediterranean.

One showed the subject sunbathing on the beach. In another he was sitting in a rowing-boat, wearing a sombrero. The four others were similar, showing him playing a guitar, buying souvenirs, preparing to dive into a swimming pool, laughing in close-up at the photographer. They conveyed the impression of a gay and happy holiday-maker and in every case the subject was the same person.

"David Walker . . ." Martin said softly, and looked up at his self-satisfied junior with a nod of approval. "Well done, Harry."

The drawing-room at Gameswood House opened out onto the garden at the back. The grass on the lawn was beginning to look untidy. It was David's practice to mow it every Sunday and nearly two weeks had passed since it had received his attention. Roy Norton had helped himself to a gin and tonic from the drinks cupboard in the corner of the room and was standing facing Evelyn across the big sofa. He was good-looking in a superficial kind of way, with the regular but somehow impersonal features of the male fashion model. He wore a suede jacket over a roll-necked pullover and trousers with a faint check pattern. Usually the embodiment of self-assurance, his veneer tended to wilt when he was under pressure, as now.

"I'm sorry, Evelyn, but if you choose to misunderstand what I've been trying to say . . ."

"Oh, come off it, Roy!" Evelyn cut in, her eyes snapping dangerously. "If you don't want to come here any more, say so and have done with it."

"It's not a question of not wanting to come here! Good heavens, I've been practically living here during the past two months. I merely said that under the present circumstances we should try and be a little more . . .well discreet."

Evelyn paced angrily towards the drinks cupboard to refill her glass. "Discreet? Isn't it a little late for that!"

"All I'm saying is that instead of meeting here, at your house, we should . . ." Roy's voice trailed off. He finished lamely: " . . .meet somewhere else occasionally."

"Where, for instance?" she said over her shoulder.

"I don't know where!" Roy finished his drink and put the glass down on the coffee table. "Look, Evelyn, I've got a rotten day ahead of me. Don't let's quarrel — not now, honey." He went up behind her, rurned her round and gave her a light kiss. "I'll pick you up this evening. Be outside my office at about half-past six."

"Let's make it earlier, about a quarter to. David's calling and I'd rather not be here when he . . ."

"David?" Surprised, Roy dropped his hands from her shoulders.

"He telephoned," Evelyn said casually. "He wants to collect some of his things. I imagine it'll be this evening some time."

"Where is he? Where's he staying?" Roy ran a hand unconsciously down the back of his head, a sure sign that he was nervous.

"He's at The Crown in Mortimer Street."

Roy started as a sharp knock sounded on the front door. His eyes darted round as if he was looking for some way to make a quick exit. "I suppose this couldn't be . . ."

"No, duckie!" Evelyn was laughing openly at his embarrassment. "I hardly think he'd knock on his own front door."

Roy groped for his cigarettes and rapidly lit up as Evelyn, quite unruffled, went out to the hall to open the door. He followed as far as the door, listening until he was certain that the voice of the visitor was not David's. He had retreated swiftly and was standing in the window embrasure when Evelyn ushered Martin Denson into the room. The Inspector was carrying a slim black attaché case.

"I apologise if I've come at an awkward moment, Mrs. Walker, but I was . . ." He broke off, feigning surprise, as he saw Roy smiling and nodding at him. "Oh! Good morning, sir."

"Mr. Norton's been giving me a driving lesson," Evelyn explained easily. She knew that the Inspector must have seen Roy's car parked outside. "He's just leaving." She turned to Roy, admonishing him with her eyes to take the hint. "This is Inspector Denson."

"Good morning." Roy gratefully moved towards the door. "I'll 'phone you about Thursday's appointment later, Mrs. Walker. I'm not quite sure how I'm placed."

"Yes; please do that," Evelyn said with formal politeness. "I'm free all day Thursday."

Martin watched impassively as Roy picked up his hat and gloves, then turned to Evelyn.

"I'm investigating a murder case, Mrs. Walker. A girl called Judy Clayton was murdered and we've reason to believe that . . ."

"Excuse me." Roy had stopped in the doorway. "Did you say — Judy Clayton?"

"Yes," said Martin, swinging round with an expression of polite enquiry.

"Is that the Judy Clayton that lives — lived — in Reigate Street?"

"Yes, that's right, sir. Did you know the young lady?"

"No. Well — yes, I knew her, but . . ." Roy came back a few steps into the room, his face worried. "When was she killed? What happened exactly?"

"We don't know what happened, except that she was murdered." Martin's voice was unemotional but his eyes never left Roy's face. "Strangled. We found her body in a ditch."

"Good God!" Roy exclaimed, genuinely shocked.

"It's been in the papers, sir," Martin said quietly. "How well did you know this girl, Mr. Norton?"

"I — hardly knew her at all. She came to my office a couple of months ago and said she was thinking of buying a car and that . . .she might possibly want some driving lessons."

"Did she have any lessons, sir?"

"No. I — I never saw her again." Roy's face was red. He looked at his watch, and feigned astonishment when he saw the time. "If you'll excuse me I — I have another appointment at ten o'clock." Evelyn moved as if to show him out, but Roy put up a hand. "It's all right, Mrs. Walker, I can let myself out."

Martin was already moving towards the settee. He placed his case on the arm and turned to face Evelyn.

"I expect you're wondering why I should want to talk to you about this affair, Mrs. Walker?"

"Yes, I am." Evelyn crossed in front of the fireplace, sat down gracefully in one of the arm-chairs and crossed her well-shaped legs. "I'm afraid I've never heard of this girl, Inspector. Judy —?"

"Clayton. Then I take it your husband never mentioned her?"

"My husband?" Evelyn's astonishment was genuine. "No. Why should he?"

"We've reason to believe he was a friend of Miss Clayton's."

"David?"

"Yes."

"That's certainly news to me, Inspector."

Martin looked down at her for a moment. She met his gaze steadily, her wide-set eyes not even blinking. She was, he reflected, just about the sexiest married woman in Guildfleet.

"Mrs. Walker, I'd like you to look at this camera and these photographs."

Martin opened the attaché case. He took out the Polaroid camera and the set of six snapshots, and handed them to her. She glanced briefly at the camera before putting it on the arm of her chair, then leafed through the photographs. Her expression had not changed when she looked up at Martin with an air of polite enquiry.

"Well?"

"Have you any idea where the photographs were taken?"

"Yes, they were taken in Italy."

"When?"

"Last year."

"What part of Italy?"

"At a place called Forte dei Marmi. It's near Viareggio."

"Have you any idea who took them?"

"I rather imagine Andy did . . ."

"Andy?"

"Andy Mason — my brother. He and David went on holiday together. We were all going but at the last moment my mother was taken ill — actually she fell downstairs and broke her leg the morning we were leaving — and I had to cry off."

"I see. And the camera?"

"What about it?"

"Have you seen it before?"

"Yes, of course I've seen it before! It's Andy's."

For the first time Martin hesitated in his questioning. "Your brother's?"

"Yes. But wait a minute!" Evelyn stared at the mirror above the mantelpiece, frowning as she tried to remember. "Surely . . .Andy lost it — he lost it at the airport in Milan." She picked the camera up and examined it with renewed interest. "But where on earth did you find it?"

"I was just going to ask the same question, Evelyn." Standing in the doorway David had been masked by Martin, who was facing Evelyn. The Inspector turned as David walked into the room. He pointed to the camera. "Where did you find it, Inspector?"

"Oh — good morning, sir," Martin said with his customary courtesy. "I'm glad you're here, I wanted to have another chat with you."

"Suppose you start by answering my question," David said uncompromisingly.

"We found the camera and the snapshots together, sir." "Yes, but where?"

Martin did not answer at once. He waited until David had moved round to a position from which he could see the snapshots. That way he could have both husband and wife in his field of vision.

"We found them in a house in Reigate Street. The house where Judy Clayton lived."

Parked in the road about a hundred yards from the entrance to Gameswood House Roy Norton had smoked three cigarettes before he saw Martin's car emerge from the gateway. He opened his door quickly, stepped out and waved to the police car to halt. Martin braked and parked his car behind the Allegro. He leaned across to open the door on the passenger side as Roy came abreast of the car. Roy threw his cigarette down before sliding in beside him.

"I've been waiting for you, Inspector. I wanted to have another word with you about . . . Judy Clayton."

"Oh?"

The monosyllabic response did not make Roy feel any more confident. He glanced uneasily at the Inspector's profile.

"It was a little awkward talking about her in front of Mrs. Walker, I mean — and obviously I didn't want her to — well — get the wrong impression."

"The wrong impression about what, sir?" Martin's tone made it clear that he was not interested in innuendos.

"About my relationship — I mean, my association with . . ." Roy broke off and sighed.

"Go on, Mr. Norton."

"Look, I'll be perfectly frank with you, Inspector." Roy squared his shoulders like Sidney Carton about to ascend the scaffold to save another's life. "I lied to you about Judy Clayton. She didn't just enquire about taking our course, she . . . As a matter of fact, she had several lessons from us."

"From you, personally?"

"Yes. Well — there you are." Having got the brief statement off his chest Roy felt relieved enough to switch on some of the old charm. "I thought you ought to know about it. It's always better to be perfectly straightforward about these things."

"Tell me about Miss Clayton," Martin said quietly. He put a hand up to adjust the driving mirror. "What sort of a person was she?"

Roy waited till a lorry loaded with ballast had churned past. "Well she was all right, I suppose. Obviously, I didn't get to know her very well."

"How many lessons did she have from you?"

"About half a dozen, I should say. She enrolled for the complete course, which is fifteen, but unfortunately she . . .well, to be honest, she refused to pay us. We just couldn't get a penny out of her."

"You surprise me, Mr. Norton. According to all accounts she was pretty well off."

"Well, that wasn't our experience. We kept sending her bills but nothing happened."

"Did you speak to her about it, personally, I mean?"

As he hesitated Roy glanced up at the driving mirror and found himself looking straight into Martin's eyes.

"Yes, I did," he said, nodding emphatically. "I bumped into her in the High Street one day and I was pretty frank with her. I said: 'You owe us twelve quid, honey. Now pay up — and no excuses, or you'll be hearing from our solicitors."

"What happened?"

"She just laughed at me."

"That's all?"

"Well, no. Just as I was leaving she said if I felt like dropping in on her one evening we could discuss the matter."

"And did you drop in on her, Mr. Norton?"

This time Martin removed his gaze from the mirror and turned his head to look at Roy directly.

"Of course I didn't!" Roy said, and laughed. "I wasn't born yesterday." Once again he ostentatiously consulted his watch and put a hand on the door catch. "If you'll excuse me, Inspector . . ."

"Just before you go," Martin said, his voice still friendly and conversational. "Do you happen to know a man called Andy Mason?"

"Andy Mason?" Roy twisted round, startled by the question. "Why, yes — he's Mrs. Walker's brother."

"Is he the man that runs The Grapevine; that pretty-looking pub near the river?"

"That's right. But he doesn't just run it; he owns the place."

"Mrs. Walker mentioned him," Martin said casually, "and I wasn't sure whether it was the same chap."

He leaned across and opened the door for Roy.

"Thank you, Mr. Norton. You've been very helpful."

Half an hour after evening opening-time the lounge bar of The Grapevine was already well populated and more customers were arriving every minute. Andy Mason had retained the old furniture, the exposed beams and the ornate Victorian furnishings of the bar, avoiding the mistake of sacrificing individuality for a spurious modern atmosphere. The room was full of the buzz of good-humoured conversation and the occasional burst of laughter. The two barmen, Mike and George, were busy drawing pints and half-pints of beer or pouring out measures from the rows of upturned bottles under the big mirror with its decorated edging.

George spotted Martin as he came in through the door and made his way to the bar. He quickly wiped a patch of spilt beer off the counter and smiled at the Inspector.

"Hello, sir! Nice to see you."

"Hello, Richards!" Martin said, surprised to be recognised.

"I didn't know you were here. How long have you been at The Grapevine?"

"About six months, sir. What can I get you, Mr. Denson?"

"I'll have a tomato juice." Martin edged sideways to make room for a hefty young man in a polo-necked sweater.

"And two gin and tonics, George," the newcomer said.

"Okay, Mr. Houghton," George said, making it clear that he intended to serve Martin first.

The young man seemed unconscious that he had pushed Martin aside. "Looks like being a full house tonight," he remarked. "Where's Olive?"

"She's in London doing a bit of shopping." George glanced round at the bar clock. "She'll be on at eight o'clock."

He turned his back to pour out Martin's tomato juice. The young man nudged the Inspector with his elbow.

"He's got a pretty face — but he's not our Olive."

Martin smiled faintly in response to the throaty laugh. He raised his eyes to the mirror behind the bar and his heart suddenly quickened its beat. He had spotted Sue sitting alone at a small table by the window.

"That'll be eight pence, Mr. Denson," George was saying to him.

Martin dragged his eyes from the mirror and groped for change. It had been a brutal shock suddenly seeing her like that in a public place. He put a coin down on the counter and while George was fetching change, turned round to watch Sue. She had a glass of sherry in front of her and was looking as attractive as ever.

"Your change, sir," George reminded him.

"Oh, thanks." Martin picked up the coin. "Is Mr. Mason about?"

"He's in the office, sir."

"Tell him I'd like a word with him if possible." He pointed towards Sue's table. "I'll be over there."

"Right, Mr. Denson," George said with a grin.

Sue had adopted the withdrawn and isolated look of a respectable woman who finds herself sitting alone in a pub. She was taking great care to avoid catching anyone's eye and so she did not realise that her former husband had come in till she looked up and saw him standing in front of her table. The remote expression rapidly changed to one of embarrassment.

"Hello, Sue!" Martin said good-humouredly. "What are you doing here?"

"I'm waiting for someone," she answered coldly.

"Is this one of your haunts?"

"No, as it happens, I've never been here before."

"Well, let me get you a drink."

She shook her head and pointed to the glass of sherry. "I've got one, thank you."

"I tried to get you on the 'phone this afternoon," Martin said, trying not to let reproachfulness creep into his voice.

"Yes, I know. I got the message. I just hadn't time to 'phone you back."

"I think it was me that got the message, Sue."

He pulled the unoccupied chair out, placed his tomato juice on the table and sat down beside her. She moved her legs, so as to avoid any risk that his knee would touch hers.

"What is it you wanted?"

"I just wanted to have a word with you about the cottage." "What about the cottage?"

Martin controlled the anger which her tone and manner were provoking, forced himself to speak in an unemotional way.

"I've heard from the estate agents. They've finally had an offer for it."

"Well?"

"I don't know whether to accept it or not."

"It's up to you," Sue said, looking the other way as she sipped at her sherry.

"Oh, Sue, come off it!" Martin exclaimed, his patience breaking.

She looked at him for the first time, tight-lipped. "Martin, it's your cottage. If you want to sell it, sell it . . ."

"All right," Martin said, suddenly flaring up. "I'll sell the bloody place and that's it!"

He swallowed his tomato juice and banged the glass down on the table. Sue studied him for a moment then seemed to relent a little.

"I don't know why you didn't sell it last year when we called it a day."

"You know perfectly well why I didn't sell it. I thought you'd . . ."

"You thought I'd come to my senses?"

He looked seriously into her eyes, and said very quietly: "I was hoping we'd both come to our senses, Sue."

The lights of a car arriving outside swung across the window and she turned her head away to avoid the glare.

"Martin, I'm perfectly happy. I've got an interesting job, a good salary, and a very cosy little bed-sitter. Now will you please do me a favour? Leave me alone . . ."

She paused and spoke the last words slowly and softly but with great emphasis. Martin knew that there was nothing more to say. He sighed and rose from the table. As he pushed the chair back a voice spoke from behind him.

"Inspector Denson?"

"Yes?"

"I'm Andy Mason. I believe you wanted a word with me?"

Andy Mason was very far from the popular conception of an innkeeper. Martin judged his age to be about thirty-five. He was almost as tall as the Inspector, but much more fragile in build. He wore a pair of dark-rimmed spectacles which gave him a vaguely studious air, an impression which was heightened by the slightly careless style of his dress — a worn tweed jacket, trousers baggy at the knees, a striped tie with a small knot slightly askew. His manner was easy and friendly but a little cautious and reserved, as if experience had taught him not to rush into friendships too rapidly.

"Yes," Martin said. "If you could spare me a few minutes?"
"Of course." Andy nodded and then smiled down at Sue. "Good evening."

Sue replied with her charming, friendly smile: "Good evening."

"What is it you want to see me about?" Andy asked Martin, without a hint of resentment or apprehension.

"I've got something I'd like you to take a look at, Mr. Mason. Perhaps we could go into your office?"

"Yes, of course."

Andy Mason turned to lead the way towards a door beside the bar. Martin lingered, hoping that he could part from Sue on a less wounding note.

"Goodbye, Sue."

There was no trace now of the smile which she had bestowed on Andy Mason. "Goodbye," she said, putting an unmistakable stress on the first syllable.

To reach Andy Mason's office they had to pass between the end of the bar and the main entrance. At that moment the door opened and a florid, buxom woman who was still good-looking and full of self-confidence came in. She had to hold the swing-door open with one hip while she manoeuvred her parcels through the gap. A customer sitting in a group near the door had gone to her help. Olive had made some suggestive comment and his friends were laughing at her reply. Mike, the second barman, lifted the flap at the end of the bar and hurried towards her.

"He meant a hand with your parcels, Olive, that's all."

Olive gave the young man, who had rejoined his friends, a broad wink. "I know what he meant, all right."

"Hello, Olive!" Andy said, laughing. "Had a good day?" He contemplated the half-dozen large parcels of which Mike was relieving her and smiled at Martin. "That's a damn silly question, isn't it? She's bought half Oxford Street, by the look of things."

Mike was pretending to be bowed down by the weight of the load. "Yes," he said to Andy. "And if you ask me she'll be wanting a sub on Thursday."

"No, I won't, Mr. Clever," Olive protested in her rich, carrying voice. "I haven't touched my wages yet." She lowered her voice and put her face closer to Andy's. "These are all on Victor."

Martin was smiling with the others at the little comedy. Before following Andy through to his office, he took a last look in Sue's direction. She was still sitting there, deep in thought, staring down at her half-finished glass of sherry.

Andy Mason's office was located directly behind the bar. The room had once been the store where the casked beer of former days had been kept. The modern furnishings which Andy had installed looked incongruous against the thick rough walls and hardly matched the solid oak beams of the ceiling. Martin was puzzled by the background noise of bar conversation which persisted even after Andy had closed the door. Then he realised it was coming from a loudspeaker behind Andy's desk. He could identify George's voice amongst the others.

Andy's desk was a litter of papers and trade macrazines.

Martin put his attache case on top of a metal filing-cabinet and snapped the catches open. Andy watched curiously as he brought out the Polaroid SX-70 camera and handed it to him.

"Is this camera familiar to you, sir?"

Andy unfastened the leather case with the ease of familiarity and extracted the camera. He turned it over, found scratches on the underside and looked up at the Inspector with a puzzled frown.

"Yes," he said. "This camera is mine. There's no doubt about it." He checked to see whether there was any film in it and then replaced it in its case. "Well, I'm damned. I certainly never thought I'd see this again."

"You say you lost it at Milan airport?"

"Yes. At least — well, I thought I did. Excuse, me, I'll turn this thing off. Sometimes I like to hear what's going on behind my back." As the switch went up the background noise was abruptly cut off. He put the camera down on his desk. "This is mine, all right. But how did you come to get hold of it, Inspector? I thought I'd lost it at Milan airport."

"We are making certain enquiries, sir," Martin said with unhelpful vagueness, "and during the course of our investigations we happened to find the camera."

"Enquiries about what — stolen property?" Andy's brow was still puckered by that mystified frown.

"No, sir." Martin's eyes had been making a lazy tour of the

room. Now they swung back to Andy and his tone became more businesslike. "Mr. Mason, tell me, what happened exactly at the airport?"

"Nothing happened, except that I was in a hell of a state." Andy gave a self-deprecating smile. "Always am when it comes to flying. Scares the pants off me. I'd had about six doubles and was just trotting off to the gents — having handed my camera and various bits and pieces over to David — when they suddenly called the flight number. The next thing I knew we were on the ruddy aircraft and I was struggling with my seat-belt."

"In fact, not to put too fine a point on it, you were pie-eyed?"

Andy laughed and nodded. "Yes, I suppose I was."

"When did you first discover the camera was missing?"

"Oh, not until the next day," Andy replied, more at ease now. "I was sorting things out and I suddenly realised I hadn't got it. I immediately rang up David and he said I'd never given it to him. In fact he said he hadn't seen it, not since we left the hotel."

"I see." Martin nodded and stood for a moment studying Andy.

The innkeeper put the camera down on top of an open copy of "I must say, I'm very glad you've found it, Inspector. It's a pretty expensive toy and it wasn't insured. But you still haven't told me where you found it?"

"Do you know a girl called Judy Clayton?"

"No, I'm afraid . . ." Andy shook his head, then pursed his lips as he looked down, thinking hard. "Judy Clayton? I know the name . . . Haven't I read something about her quite recently?" He snapped his fingers. "Good God, I remember! Surely — she's the girl that was murdered?"

"That's right, sir," Martin agreed equably.

"Well, what's Judy Clayton got to do with my camera?"

"We found it in her bedroom, sir. In a cupboard."

"But how in heaven's name did she get hold of it?"

"I can't imagine. Unless, of course, she was a friend of Mr. Walker's and he gave it to her."

"That's absurd, Inspector!" Andy exclaimed with emphasis.

"Why, sir?" Martin asked in his innocently quiet voice. "Because in the first place David wouldn't steal the camera, and in the second place . . ." Andy bit off whatever he had been going to say, took his spectacles off and began to polish them with his handkerchief.

"Go on," Martin prompted.

"In the second place," Andy said, choosing his words, "he certainly wouldn't be friendly with a girl like Judy Clayton." "You mean — he's just not that sort of chap."

"That's exactly what I mean. But haven't you met him?"

"Yes, I have. And he's your brother-in-law, sir, isn't he? I'd like to hear your opinion of him."

Andy got his glasses back on again and looked the Inspector straight in the eye. "Well, I can give it to you in ten seconds flat. He's loyal, honest and a damn good husband. If you ask me, a great deal better than my sister deserves."

Martin had his evening meal at a small restaurant at the other end of Guildfleet from his flat and was home at a little after eight-thirty. As always, he felt a sense of depression as he let himself into an apartment which he knew was empty. He hung up his overcoat in the hall and put the attaché case on the floor by the sofa. There were enough papers in it to keep him occupied until midnight. He took a can of beer from the fridge, opened it and carefully poured the half-pint into a tilted glass.

He was looking through the long-playing records scattered on the table, trying to choose one which would not distract him from his work, when the door bell sounded shrilly. He put his beer down and went through the hall to open the door.

His visitor, having got so far as ringing the bell, must have had second thoughts, for as Martin looked out onto the landing she was already at the top of the stairs. She turned, realising that she had gone beyond the point of no return and came slowly back.

"Good evening, Inspector Denson," she said nervously.

Martin smiled reassuringly at the slightly comic figure. She was a stout woman who would never see fifty again, with a triple chin and pink, chubby cheeks. Her eyes, which were small but remarkably sharp and observant, had been touched up with a shading of mascara. She had evidently put on her best clothes, presumably from some deep wardrobe where mothballs had preserved them since a past decade. Most incongruous of all, she wore a hat decorated with plastic flowers which would have been more suitable for an afternoon on the sward at Ascot.

"Good evening," Martin responded guardedly, then suddenly recognised her. "Oh, hello, Mrs. Bodley. I'm sorry I didn't recognise you."

"It's the hat, I'm afraid, it . . ." She touched it with a trembling hand. "Could you spare me a few minutes, Inspector?"

"Yes, of course. By all means." Martin held his door wide open. "Come along in!"

As he ushered Judy Clayton's landlady into his sitting-room he suddenly realised how untidy the room was. Her sharp little eyes darted about disapprovingly, noting the books on the sofa, the scattered record sleeves, the dust on the shelves and at least two dirty tea or coffee cups.

Martin went past her, scooped up some books which were cluttering the sofa and put them on the floor.

"Sit down, Mrs. Bodley. I was just getting myself a drink. Would you care for one?"

"No, thank you, sir." Mrs. Bodley shook her head primly and the plastic flowers quivered. But she carefully lowered her broad person onto the low settee.

"Well, what can I do for you?"

"I — I owe you an apology, Inspector. The other day, when you came to the house, I —" She broke off and then looked up at him directly. "Well, I'm afraid I wasn't very helpful."

"No, but it was understandable," Martin said soothingly. "The murder must have been a great shock."

"Yes, it was." Mrs. Bodley shook her head and sighed deeply. "A great shock. I — I just couldn't believe it. Even now sometimes I . . ."

"What is it you want to tell me, Mrs. Bodley?" Martin picked up his beer and sat down in a chair facing her.

"I saw a Mr. Revelwhite this morning, I don't know whether you know him or not? He's a solicitor . . ."

"Yes, I know him. 'Revelwhite and Tucker' in Mortimer Street."

"That's right. Horace Revelwhite's an old friend of mine, I've known him for years."

"They're a very good firm." Martin put the glass to his lips and lowered the level by one third.

"I went to see him about a property I've just sold. There's some trouble over the . . ." She waved the matter away with a be-ringed hand. "Anyway, we started talking about the murder, about Judy Clayton. I said you'd questioned me and that I'd been rather, well . . ."

Martin smiled. "Rather difficult?"

"Yes!" she said, relieved that this was proving less difficult than she'd expected. "To cut a long story short he told me to come along here and apologise."

"I'll bet he also told you not to be such an obstinate old hen in future!"

"That's exactly what he told me!" Mrs. Bodley gave vent to a deep-throated, wheezing chuckle. "Those were his exact words."

"I know Horace Revelwhite — and I'm very grateful to him." Martin had put on his most serious expression. "We need all the help we can get, Mrs. Bodley. If you know anything about Judy Clayton, anything which you think might interest the police, please tell me."

She pursed her lips, hesitating, as if she was not sure whether she should speak her mind or not. When she spoke it was in a low-ered, confidential tone.

"The only thing I can tell you is, she had lots of friends — boy friends, I mean — and she was certainly never short of money."

"Tell me about the boy friends."

"Well." She looked down at her shoes, still not entirely happy about what she was doing. "There was a chap called Norton — Roy Norton."

"He runs a driving school," Martin put in, to help her along.

"That's right. He was very friendly with her — oh, for about

44

six months. Then suddenly, I don't quite know why, it was broken off."

Her mouth stayed open after she had spoken and she stared out through the uncurtained window.

"Go on, Mrs. Bodley."

"Shortly after that there was another man . . . Now what on earth was his name?" She scratched the side of her thigh to prod her memory. "He never came to the house but she was crazy about him; always rushing up to London to meet him. I bumped into the pair of them at the theatre one night and she introduced me to him . . . Now what the devil did she say his name . . .?" Her eyes were exploring the room, searching for information. They found it improbably enough, on the sleeve of Martin's recording of the Gondoliers. "Mason! That's it! Andy Mason."

"Andy Mason?" Martin was surprised, but his face showed nothing. "Are you sure that was the name?"

"Yes, I'm quite sure," Mrs. Bodley affirmed, forgetting her hesitation of a moment before.

"He owns The Grapevine — that pretty little pub near the river."

"I wouldn't know about that." She shook her head self-righteously, as if owning a pub was something faintly indecent. "All I know is, she was very friendly with him."

"Mr. Mason has a brother-in-law, a man called David Walker."

"Yes, the Sergeant mentioned him."

Martin put his glass down, stood up and went to retrieve his attaché case from the floor beside Mrs. Bodley's chubby legs.

"We're very interested in Mr. Walker. He gave Judy Clayton a lift in his car, the day she was murdered. But there are other reasons why we're interested in him, Mrs. Bodley." He pressed the catches which snapped open with a sharp crack. "Was David Walker a friend of Judy Clayton's?"

She contemplated the case on Martin's knee with some apprehension. "No, I don't think so; she certainly never mentioned him. But he might have been, of course. She invited quite a lot of people

45

to the house at one time or another. I don't suppose I even saw half of them. What does this David Walker look like?"

"Well, when he's on holiday, he looks like this." Martin had taken the big white envelope from his case. He selected one of the snapshots and handed it to Mrs. Bodley. She gave it only the briefest glance and then looked up.

"But this is the man I told you about! The one I was introduced to." Her face expressed complete bewilderment. She held the snapshot closer and stared at it again. "The man she said was Andy Mason!"

It was a good deal later that night when Roy Norton's Jaguar — his personal car, not the hack he used for driving lessons — turned into the drive at Gameswood House. The frosty silence had continued all the way from The Bear Hotel. The bottle of Burgundy and Chateaubriand steak which they had shared in the grill-room of Guildfleet's most expensive establishment had done nothing at all to improve Evelyn Walker's temper.

Roy stopped the car in front of the door and switched the engine off. In view of their agreement not to use Gameswood House for their meetings any longer he knew that she would not be inviting him in, but he wanted to try and get things straight before they separated. Her attitude was so unfair. She seemed to think he had nothing to do except dance attendance on her. If he had not found her so damnably desirable he'd have broken this thing off long ago, but he knew now that he was well and truly hooked. It wasn't love in the proper sense, more like some delicious addiction.

"I really am sorry about tonight, Evelyn. I didn't realise it would take me so long."

She tossed her head petulantly. "I felt such an idiot sitting there on my own."

"Yes, I know. I'm sorry, honey." Roy put an arm round her shoulders and tried to draw her against him. She pushed his arm away and slid further from him.

"I still don't see why you couldn't have 'phoned from the hotel. Rushing back to your office like that in the middle of a meal!"

"I've told you, I couldn't remember her number and the silly old cow isn't in the book, so I . . ." He took her hands and pulled her round to face him. "Look, Evelyn, I'm sorry — I apologise. Now let's forget it, honey."

Abruptly her mood changed. She moved closer, allowing his arm to slip caressingly round her shoulders.

"All right, but promise you won't do it again?"

"Of course I won't do . . ."

She twisted round to look into his face, her expression teasing, almost mocking. "Promise? Cross your heart and hope to die?"

"Yes, of course I promise!"

Her lips were parted and moist. He bent his head and gave her a long kiss. She broke away just as he felt the desire growing in him, and put her hand on the door catch.

"I'll give you a ring tomorrow sometime — probably in the afternoon."

"Okay, darling," Roy said, trying to hide his frustration. She banged the door. He gave her a wave and started the engine.

Evelyn watched the tail lights disappear through the gate as she felt in her handbag for her keys. It had been daylight when she left the house and so it was in complete darkness. She felt no apprehension as she opened the door and entered the dark hall. She knew exactly where to find the switches. Her movements were decisive as she turned on the hall lights, shrugged off her fur coat and threw it over a chair. She moved on to the drawing-room, pausing at the door to snap down all the switches and flood the room with light. She crossed quickly to the windows and pulled the cords that drew the curtains across.

In the short space of time since she had parted from Roy her manner had completely changed. The girlish petulance and teasing playfulness had vanished. She had already completely dismissed her admirer from her mind and looked more like the female director of a business school than a driving instructor's mistress.

For a moment she stood still in the middle of the room, her face hard as she concentrated her thoughts. She glanced at her watch and then moved purposefully over to the sofa drawn up at right angles to the fireplace. The telephone was on the small table beside it. She picked up the instrument, dialled three digits, and waited impatiently till the operator answered.

"International Service, please," she said crisply. "United States."

This time the delay was shorter before the international operator answered.

"International Service. What country, please?"

"I want to send a cable to New York . . . My number's Guild-fleet 701 . . . The subscriber's name is Walker . . . The cable's for a Mr. Jack Stenhouse . . . Yes, that's right, Stenhouse . . . Waldorf Astoria Hotel, Park Avenue, New York . . . Please telephone me ten o'clock tomorrow night. Must talk to you. All my love. Evelyn . . . That's right . . . EVELYN."

It was as she stood listening to the operator reading the message back to her that she became really aware of a shiny object which lay on the small table. It was David's cigarette case and it was open, as if he had been surprised while filling it from the large silver cigarette box.

When the message ended she thanked the operator tersely, put the receiver down and thoughtfully picked up the case. Suddenly she spun round, as if she half expected to find David coming through the door, as he had done that day when Inspector Denson had been here.

The house was very quiet as she went out into the hall. Somewhere a board creaked and the big grandfather clock tickered as it always did a few seconds before striking. She went to the foot of the stairs and called softly: "David?"

There was no light on upstairs. Her throat had tightened and she knew her voice had been faint. She tried again, more loudly.

"David, are you upstairs?"

The grandfather clock gathered its strength and struck eleven solemn notes. They echoed eerily through the house. As she turned to re-enter the drawing-room she noticed that the door of David's study was half open. It had been closed when she went out; in fact that door had not been opened since David had gone to live at The Crown.

She went to the door and pushed it wide. David hated overhead lights. All the table lamps, including the one on his desk, were wired to switch on at the door. The switch she found first was the desk lamp.

She drew in her breath so quickly that the air hissed between her lips and she instinctively closed her eyes. It took her perhaps ten seconds to recover from the shock and regain control of herself. Then she pressed down the remaining switches and walked slowly into the room, circling the desk till she was standing behind it.

There was no question that he was dead. It must have been instantaneous the moment the bullet from the small-calibre automatic entered his temple. His head had crashed forward onto the desk, splattering blood over the papers. The hand gripping the gun in the spasm of death splayed across the green leather top. Mercifully his face was hidden.

Her eyes scanned the desk rapidly, noting and memorising the letters and documents, the tray for pens and pencils, the pipe-rack, a silver cigarette lighter and the portable typewriter — this last had been pushed to one side. A single sheet of paper, neatly and carefully typed, had been laid on top of it.

She looked at it for a moment then picked it up and held it under the lamp. The half-dozen lines in the middle of the page caught her immediate attention.

" . . . I killed Judy Clayton and in the end I had no alternative but to kill myself. For some time now I've been having an affair with Judy. One night, about six months ago, she started to blackmail me . . ."

She glanced at the dead body of her husband. Her expression was one of annoyance, almost frustration. Then she straightened up, listening. She was almost certain that she had heard a car turning in and stopping at the front of the house. She was still holding the paper in her hand. On a sudden impulse she picked up the lighter and flipped the bevelled cylinder to ignite the flame. It failed to light. She tried again and as the flame spurted up a sharp double knock sounded on the front door.

There was something urgent and commanding about that

knock echoing through the empty house. The knocker must have been wielded by an authoritative hand. She froze, uncertain what to do, the flame held a few inches from the corner of the suicide note. Then she snapped the lighter shut, put it back on the desk and replaced the sheet on top of the typewriter where she had found it.

Totally in command of herself, she moved at an unhurried pace towards the door of the study.

Chapter Two

"Perhaps she's gone to bed," Kennedy suggested. "Shall I try the knocker?"

"The hall lights are on," Martin pointed out. "And anyway, it's only just gone eleven o'clock."

After Christine Bodley had left him, Martin dug Detective-Sergeant Kennedy from his digs and told him that they were going to interview David Walker. To their surprise the Manager of The Crown told them that David had settled his bill earlier that evening and moved out. Martin had decided to try Gameswood House on the off-chance that he had gone home to try and patch things up with his wife. It was astonishing how often married couples, after an apparently final break, will fall into each other's arms again.

Kennedy's hand was already on the knocker when Martin put a hand on his arm. Through the door he had heard the tap of a woman's heels on the parquet flooring inside. A second later the door was opened. Evelyn Walker stood there, the light behind her so that her face was in shadow. Even so, something about the droop of her shoulders and the limp way her arms hung at her sides warned Martin.

"Good evening, Mrs. Walker. Is your husband here by any —"

She had put one hand against her brow and with the other was groping for support against the door frame.

"What is it?" Martin shot a quick glance at Kennedy, who moved forward. "What's happened?"

"My husband's — dead." She spoke in the flat voice of someone who is still in shock. "He's — he's committed suicide —"

Abruptly her arms dropped limply again and her knees began to buckle. Kennedy, already on the move, was in time to catch her and prevent her inert body from slumping onto the stone steps. He swept her off her feet and held her in his arms, one hand hanging and her head drooping over his forearm.

"Take her into the house," Martin told him. He followed Kennedy in and closed the door. "The drawing-room will do."

The Inspector had noted that the lights in the drawing-room were full on. He entered before the laden Kennedy and his eyes quickly surveyed the room, his keen sense of smell picking up the tang of a recently-smoked cigarette. The cigarette case lying open on the table by the telephone caught his attention. He went over and looked down at it without touching it.

"You'd better stay with her," he told Kennedy, who had deposited Evelyn on the sofa.

He went out into the hall, mentally bracing himself to face whatever he was going to find. Suicides seldom made as clean a job of killing themselves as they hoped. The lights burning in the study opposite told him that he would not have to look far.

Three minutes later Kennedy found him standing behind the body slumped over the desk, the suicide note held in his hand. The eyes of the two men met, but they said nothing. Even for a policeman it always took a little while to adjust to the spectacle of violent death. Kennedy walked into the room slowly, taking care not to move or disturb any object till the photographers had recorded the scene.

After a minute Martin looked up, his face bleak.

"How is she?"

"Not too bad, considering. It must have been a hell of a shock finding him like this." Kennedy nodded at the body. "How long do you think he's been dead?"

"Not long, I should say. But that's only a guess. We'll see what the doctor says."

"Apparently she didn't even know he was in the house." Kennedy noted Martin's sceptical expression. He went on: "She suddenly saw his cigarette case on the table in the lounge and went to look for him."

"I see," Martin commented in a non-commital voice. "Right, Harry. Get the station to lay things on. Oh, and ask them to call The Grapevine and tell Andy Mason what's happened. I expect he'll want to be with his sister."

"Right." Kennedy moved towards the door. "I'll use the 'phone in the hall."

Martin read the note through once more. Then he took an envelope from his pocket, folded the note and placed it inside. He put the envelope in his pocket and with another quick glance round the study went across to the drawing-room.

Evelyn was sitting up on the settee, bent forward with her head in her hands. She seemed unaware of Martin's presence as he stood before her looking down on to her dishevelled blonde hair. He was on the verge of saying something, then changed his mind. His eyes had located the drinks cupboard on his first visit to the house. He crossed towards it, found a bottle of whisky, poured a small measure into a glass and added a little water.

When he turned back he found that she was looking at him, her lips working and tears misting her eyes. He handed her the glass.

"You'd better drink this, Mrs. Walker."

"Thank you." She took the glass gingerly. He stood watching her as she sipped the drink.

"I'm sorry to worry you at a time like this, but I'm afraid there are one or two questions I've got to ask you."

She dabbed at her eyes with a handkerchief, and seemed to make an effort to put a brave face on it.

"I'd — I'd rather tell you now anyway, and get it over with."

"Tell me what, Mrs. Walker?"

"My husband committed suicide because he . . ." She broke off, closed her eyes tight in mental pain, then continued with evident distress and difficulty. " . . .found out . . . I've been having an affair with Roy Norton. David came home early from the office one afternoon and we . . . Roy and I . . . were upstairs and . . ." She put a hand to her brow again and her mouth trembled.

"I don't think it's quite as simple as that, Mrs. Walker," Martin said, very reasonably and quietly.

She looked up sharply, a sudden alertness in her eyes. "What do you mean?"

"Your husband left a note . . ."

"A note?"

"It was addressed to his partner, Arthur Eastwood. The note said he'd been friendly with Judy Clayton — the girl I spoke to you about — and that she'd been blackmailing him."

"David?" She shook her head emphatically. "I can't believe that!"

"I'm only telling you what's in the note. It said she'd been blackmailing him and because of that . . . he killed her."

"He . . ." Evelyn appeared to be stunned by the statement. "I don't believe it! I — I just don't believe it!"

"Why don't you believe it?"

"Because David wasn't like that," she told him indignantly, "and if he'd been friendly with anyone I'd have known about it."

"Would you, Mrs. Walker?" Martin paused before putting the question. "When did you last see your husband?"

"This morning — you were here. He came to collect his things."

"Did he say he might possibly be returning for something, later in the day?"

She finished the drink. Martin bent to take the glass from her. He took it back to the drinks cupboard.

"No," she said, watching him with a worried frown. "He simply told me what I already knew. That he was staying at The Crown and if I wanted to get in touch with him I could ring the office."

"Have you been in touch with him — since this morning, I mean?"

"No." She put the handkerchief to her eyes again and struggled for a moment to control herself. "No, I haven't."

Martin sat down in the armchair on the opposite side of the fireplace. Kennedy had had the good sense to switch on the imitation coal fire.

"Tell me about this evening, Mrs. Walker. What time was it when you left the house?"

"It was about six o'clock. Roy — Mr. Norton — picked me up outside his office and drove over to Chertsey to see some friends."

"Go on."

"We had a few drinks with them and then we drove back to Guildfleet and had dinner at The Bear."

"Just the two of you?"

"Yes."

"What time would that be?"

"It was about half-past seven when we got there." She had recovered her composure now and was speaking with more assurance. "I don't know what time it was when we left, probably about ten o'clock."

"And Mr. Norton brought you home, presumably?"

"Yes," she said and then added quickly: "but he didn't come in the house —" She stopped, having obviously remembered something. She was sufficiently in control of herself now to give him a weak smile. "Inspector, would you do something for me? Would you telephone my brother and tell him what's happened?"

"That's already been taken care of," Martin reassured her. He had been observing her performance with interest and not a little admiration. "Just one more question, Mrs. Walker. Was Mr. Norton with you the entire evening from the moment he picked you up until he brought you home?"

"Why, yes." Her eyes had widened innocently. "Yes, of course."

"Thank you." Martin stood up and offered her a hand to help her rise. "Now I suggest you go upstairs and lie down for a little while, Mrs. Walker. I'll let you know the moment your brother gets here."

If Martin's flat had aroused the disapproval of the tidy-minded Christine Bodley, his office at the Guildfeet Police Station would have brought a beam of approval to her generously fleshed face. The morning sunlight slanting through the clear window panes brought reflections from the well-polished desk, filing cabinet and cupboard.

The most untidy object in the room, in fact, was Martin's

guest. Arthur Eastwood was sitting uncomfortably on the single leather easy-chair, which was so slippery that his bottom kept sliding forward. He looked tired and dejected and his tweed suit was more crumpled than ever. He was staring at the note which had been left on David's typewriter, holding it at arm's length to compensate for his long-sightedness.

"But this note's typed and the signature could be anybody's!" he protested.

Seated behind his desk, Martin leaned forward to retrieve the note which Arthur Eastwood had put on the far edge.

"That's not what you said a moment ago when I first showed it to you. You said . . ."

"I said it like his signature. Well — it does, I suppose. But damn it all, one word — 'David'. Anybody could copy that! I could do it myself?"

Arthur put his hands on the arms of the chair to heave himself into a more upright position.

"So you don't think he was responsible for the note?"

"No, I don't! I don't think he typed it, I don't think he signed it, and I don't think he committed suicide! And what's more, I don't think you think so either!"

"Well, one thing we do know, his death certainly wasn't an accident, so if he didn't commit suicide there's only one alternative. Murder." Martin refolded the note, replaced it in its envelope and put it away in one of his desk drawers. "We have a motive for suicide, but I doubt very much whether we have a motive for murder. Have you any idea why anyone should want to murder him?"

"No." Mention of murder had shocked Arthur. Now the Inspector had used the word three times and each time Arthur had reacted with a tremor of the flesh round his eyes. "No, I haven't. I just can't imagine why. . . ."

He broke off as Martin pushed his chair back, moved out from behind his desk and went to lean with one elbow on the filing cabinet.

"Mr. Eastwood, what happens in your business when you

have a hunch about something, yet all the available facts seem to make nonsense of it?"

"I lose sleep."

Martin had to smile at Eastwood's gloomy admission. "Yes, well — if it's any consolation to you, I'm losing sleep right now."

"What does that mean, Inspector?"

"It means that although I sympathise with your feelings, although there's a doubt in my mind about . . ."

"About whether he committed suicide?"

"Yes. The fact speak for themselves. And the facts tell us, quite clearly, that David Walker knew Judy Clayton. That he knew her long before he picked her up in his car last Tuesday morning."

Arthur shook his head. "I'm sorry, I don't go along with that. So far as I'm concerned, that's just supposition."

"Well, if it's supposition, how do you account for her having the key-ring? Do you really think she stole it? How do you account for the fact that she had photographs of him in a cabinet by the side of her bed? And how do you account for the fact that she actually had an appointment to meet someone that morning — at ten-thirty, at precisely the spot where David Walker picked her up?"

The battery of questions had reduced Arthur to complete silence. He dropped his eyes to the floor and put his hands on his knees.

"I still don't think he knew her," he persisted doggedly, and pushed himself to his feet, "and I still don't think he committed suicide."

Martin turned as knuckles rapped sharply on the door. A police clerk in uniform came in with a fistful of documents. Martin watched with resignation as P.C. Reeves put the pile on his desk. There would be at least two hours' work in that lot, he thought.

"Tell Sergeant Kennedy I'd like a word with him," he told Reeves as the clerk was leaving.

"I'm afraid he's out, sir." Reeves glanced at Arthur then back at Martin. "Mrs. Bodley, Judy Clayton's landlady, 'phoned and said she wanted to see him."

"When was this?"

"About an hour ago, sir."

Martin nodded dismissal and the door closed on P.C. Reeves. He sat down at his desk again and picked up the top paper on the pile. It was the post mortem report on David Walker.

Arthur, who had been hoping to make his escape, pricked up his ears as Martin read aloud the key sentences from the report.

"Death must have been instantaneous because there seems to be little doubt that the bullet penetrated' . . . Yes, well we know the cause of death all right . . . 'As far as I ascertain, Mr. Walker died between eight and nine o'clock' . . ." He looked up at Arthur. "Let's say eight — that's about two hours after you 'phoned him at The Crown."

"Yes." Arthur had started to nod agreement. Then his jaw dropped. "But . . . I didn't mention any 'phone call . . ."

Martin agreed smilingly. "I know you didn't. But I understand you made one. Tell me about the call, sir. Did Mr. Walker sound perfectly normal?"

"Yes." Arthur's voice was slightly resentful, as if he felt that he was being spied on. "So far as I could tell he appeared to be the same as usual. We had quite a lengthy discussion."

"About what, sir?"

Arthur hesitated, then decided to sit down in the slippery chair again. "Well, very much between ourselves, Inspector, the Stenhouse Corporation are trying to buy us out. I spent a couple of hours in London yesterday afternoon discussing the deal and — well, that's what David and I talked about."

"I see. Mr. Walker didn't mention his wife at all?"

"No. There was no reason why he should."

"Mrs. Walker isn't concerned with the business? She's not involved in the takeover in any way?"

"No, not at all. Although . . ." Arthur paused, startled at the thought which Martin's question had planted in his mind. "I don't quite know what's going to happen now, of course. I imagine she'll inherit his shares, in which case . . ." He gave a deep sigh. "Anyhow, we can cross that bridge when we come to it."

Martin nodded. He swung his chair sideways and crossed his legs. It was somehow a more friendly and informal attitude.

"It's really no business of mine, sir, so forgive my asking but — would you say Mr. Walker was a wealthy man?"

"It depends what you mean by wealthy, of course." Arthur gave him a straight look and nodded. "But yes, I'd say he was wealthy."

"Thank you, Mr. Eastwood." Arthur waited, but to his surprise the Inspector seemed to have no more questions. He stood up and Martin did the same. They were half way to the door when Martin seemed to remember something. "Oh, there's just one point, sir. Did Mr. Walker tell you he was leaving the hotel?"

"No, he didn't."

"And yet soon after your 'phone call he paid his bill and checked out."

"Yes, and I find that very odd . . ." Arthur stopped. He resented the way Martin threw these questions at him, catching him unawares.

"Go on, sir."

"Well, just before I rang off I said to him: 'How are you, David? Are you comfortable?"

"And what did he say?"

"He said: 'Yes, I'm fine, Arthur. They're looking after me very well here."

"I see."

Martin was looking at him with his thoughtful blue eyes when the door was opened and Sergeant Kennedy came in. He was wearing his overcoat and his face was flushed, either from the wind or suppressed excitement.

"I'm sorry, sir, I thought . . ."

"That's all right. Come in. You know Mr. Eastwood?" "Good morning, Sergeant."

"I'll be with you in a minute," Martin told his assistant, and ushered Arthur Eastwood out into the corridor.

Kennedy swiftly drew from his overcoat pocket a thick wad of banknotes, held together by a wide rubber band. He put them on the corner of the desk and had just time to remove his overcoat and hang it up before the Inspector returned.

"Well, what did Mrs. Bodley want?"

Kennedy, with the expression of an amateur conjurer who is about to produce his first rabbit from a top-hat, contented himself with pointing towards the wad of notes.

"Good Lord!" Martin stared at the notes in disbelief. "What have you done — robbed a bank? How much is there?"

Kennedy, watching his chiefs face carefully, grinned with pleasure at his reaction.

"Three hundred quid. Mrs. Bodley found the money under Judy Clayton's mattress. The notes were apparently intended for a friend of hers. Someone called Victor."

The Sergeant moved across and picked up the wad again. He held it so that Martin could see the small piece of paper inserted under the elastic. The name 'Victor' had been scribbled on it.

"Victor," Martin repeated, scratching his chin. "I've heard that name before. Quite recently."

"When Mrs. Bodley told me about the money, I had an idea." Kennedy's young face had adopted its 'great detective' expression. "A theory, in fact. You know what I think?"

"No," Martin answered automatically. He was still trying to locate that name in his mind and was not really listening to the Sergeant.

"David Walker was telling the truth. Judy Clayton black-mailing him, but not on her own. It's my bet she was working for somebody, somebody called Victor. It's my bet she received instructions from this man and every so often . . ." He stopped and glared at the Inspector accusingly. "You're not listening to me! You haven't heard a word I've said!"

"I've got it!" Martin exclaimed. "Olive — the barmaid at The Grapevine! That's where I heard the name Victor! I knew damn well I . . ." He put a hand on Kennedy's arm and gripped it. "Harry, get your coat!"

"What do you mean, get it?" Kennedy was still feeling hurt at the scant attention given to his theory. "It's there! On the peg."

"I'll buy you a drink," Martin said, steering him towards the coat rack. "I might even buy you a sandwich."

"You're on!" Kennedy replied swiftly. "And it's going to be smoked salmon!"

Like many innkeepers whose trade had been hit when the breathalyser was introduced Andy Mason had tried to recoup the lost income by serving snacks. It had turned out to be such a good thing that he had kept it up, even when the motoring public had reconciled itself to living — and drinking — with the new law. A good many Guildfleet people made a regular habit of lunching at The Grapevine and at mid-day one end of the lounge bar was set aside for those who wanted to eat their food sitting down. Martin and Kennedy were ensconced at a table in the corner congratulating themselves on having got there early enough to secure a table. The place was rapidly filling up.

Kennedy's face brightened as he saw the opulent form of Olive making her way towards them with a tray.

"There isn't any smoked salmon left, I'm afraid," she said, standing in front of their table. "I've brought you ham and tongue. I hope that's all right?"

The Sergeant's face fell, but Martin nodded with a grin. "Yes, that's fine."

"You said a pint of bitter?"

"That's right," said Kennedy. "Thank you."

She put the tankard in front of him and put the sandwiches down between the two men.

"And what was yours? You said a tonic water, but you must mean a gin and tonic."

"No," Martin said. "Just a plain tonic, Olive."

"You're sure it won't go to your head?"

Martin laughed. "You keep cracks like that for that wealthy boy friend of yours!"

Olive, who had started back towards the bar to fetch Martin's drink, turned to look at him scornfully.

"Are you kidding? If I had a wealthy boy friend I wouldn't be on this lark!"

"Come off it, Olive! I was here the other night when you got back from Town — you were loaded with parcels!" Martin gave Kennedy a wink. "This boy friend of her's took her up to London, bought her half Oxford Street, and then . . ."

"What d'you mean, took me up to London!" Olive protested. "I took myself up! And those presents you're on about were on dear old Victor."

"I know. It's Victor I'm talking about, Olive."

Olive stared at him for a moment, completely non-plussed. Then she put her head back and gave a rich, throaty laugh which made half the men in the bar look round.

"What's the joke?" Kennedy asked, when she paused to wipe her eyes.

Olive, speaking loudly enough to share the joke with everyone within earshot, announced: "For your information, Mr. Know-all, Victor has long ears and four legs and he came in at eight to one! And thank God he did!"

Still laughing, she presented her back and began to push her way to the bar. Kennedy, seeing Martin's expression of discomfiture, burst out laughing himself.

"A horse!"

"Yes." Martin's face was suddenly serious. He lowered his voice and leaned closer to Kennedy. "This afternoon check every betting shop in Guildfleet, in the county if necessary."

"Why?" The Sergeant's mirth was checked when he realised what kind of an afternoon lay ahead of him. "Why do that, for Pete's sake?"

"I want to know if Judy Clayton played the horses."

It was half-past five and the civilian clerical staff were going off duty before Kennedy at last showed up in Martin's office. He was looking tired but satisfied.

"Any luck?" Martin asked, getting up from his desk. "Yes. Your hunch was right."

The Sergeant took off his overcoat and hung it up. Then he sat down in the leather arm-chair, put his notebook on the arm and placed a newspaper, open at the sporting page, on his knees.

"I checked both the betting shops in Guildfleet and then in every town within a radius of ten miles. Nearly all of them recognised her photo. She must have made a packet during the past twelve months. And if she'd put that three hundred on Victor . . ."

"Which was obviously the intention," Martin interposed. ". . . she'd have really cleaned up."

Martin perched himself on the end of his desk and contemplated his assistant with approval. "Well, she certainly knew how to pick winners."

"Somebody did," Kennedy said, with heavy emphasis. "What does that mean?"

"I found out something." The Sergeant flipped open his notebook. "Something that will really interest you. Of course, it may be just a coincidence."

"Let's have it."

"Six months ago Judy Clayton backed a horse called Fairmount. It won the Arlington Stakes. The odds were six to one. At the time, Fairmount was owned and trained by a man called Reams — Colonel Reams."

"Go on."

Kennedy consulted his notebook, running his index finger under the neatly written entries as he proceeded.

"Two weeks after winning five hundred pounds on Fairmount she put sixty quid on a horse called Jester's Cap — a rank outsider. Ridden by Fred Clarke, trained by Colonel Reams, it ran in the Winstanely Stakes at Newmarket — ran being the understatement of the year. It romped home at thirty to one."

"Good God!" Martin murmured.

Kennedy closed his notebook, satisfied now that he had really astonished the Inspector.

"To my knowledge she's had six winners during the past eight months and, with one exception, every horse had been trained by the same man."

"Colonel Reams?"

"Yes."

"Who is this Colonel Reams?"

"He lives near Guildfleet, but his racing stables are on Kingswood Downs."

"Kingswood Downs? But that's very near the spot where . . ."

"Where David Walker picked up Judy Clayton," Kennedy finished the sentence for him. "Yes, I know. I said you'd be interested."

Sergeant Kennedy, at the wheel of the CID car, slowed virtuously as he approached the 'Yield' sign at the Golden Swan crossroads. The Inspector, who was in the passenger seat beside him was a stickler for the police driving code. He waited till the major road was clear then accelerated across. The road soon began to climb gently as it wound its way through the predominantly agricultural countryside. Ahead and to the right the low profile of Kingswood Downs rose above the cultivated fields.

The entrance to Colonel Reams' training stables was easy to identify by the white-painted ranch-style fencing on either side of the gates. A well-kept drive led to the buildings, which stood half a mile back from the road. In the fields on either side aristocratic-looking race-horses were grazing, their coats glistening in the morning sun. Kennedy stopped the car opposite a square yard, lined on three sides with stables and open on the fourth. Opposite, again enclosed with gleaming white fencing, was the paddock.

The heads of a dozen horses, looking out over the tops of their stable doors, turned curiously towards the car. In front of one open door a young woman was just in the act of throwing a saddle over a horse. She was wearing a black sweater and a well-cut pair of riding breeches. As she looked round to see who the intruders were, Kennedy's lips were forming to give a low whistle of appreciation.

"Good heavens!" Martin exclaimed. "I think it's Ruth Jensen!"

"Do you know her?" Kennedy asked with a touch of envy.

"Yes, I was at school with her husband. He died about two years ago."

The Sergeant's eyes had not left the trim figure of the girl, who was stooping to tighten the girths.

"Quite a pretty girl."

"Yes, she's a great friend of Sue's," Martin said, with a hand on the door catch. "You wait here."

Martin got out of the car and took a look around to give himself an idea of the general layout of the place. A group of low buildings, which probably contained the offices, lay a hundred yards beyond the stables. As he walked towards her, the girl finished fastening the straps. She gave the horse a pat on the neck and turned to meet Martin. Immediately her wind-tanned face broke into a smile of welcome. Martin took off his hat, and returned her smile.

"Ruth Jensen, of all people! What are you doing here?" Ruth laughed. "I was just going to say the same thing!" Martin went up to her and gave her a friendly kiss on the cheek. "I'm looking for the man who owns this place — Colonel Reams."

"He's my boss." Ruth jerked her head towards the low buildings he had noticed. "You'll find him in the office."

"But how long have you been here, Ruth? I thought Sue told me you were working in London."

"I was, for a time, but I got fed up with it. I couldn't stand the journey every day. I've been here about eighteen months now." "As long as that?"

Ruth met his eyes and her mouth dropped a little at the corners. "Yes, it's over three years since Phil died, you know."

"Really? Good heavens, I'd no idea it was that long."

For a moment she stared unseeingly across the paddock, then smiled again and changed the subject. "How's Sue? Have you seen her recently?"

"Yes, I saw her the other day," Martin said casually, "just for a few minutes. She appears to be all right."

"I was sorry, Martin, when I heard," she hesitated, trying to find words that would not sound too brutal, "what had happened."

He shrugged. "It was inevitable, I'm afraid. I don't blame Sue — I don't blame myself even — it just didn't work out, Ruth."

65

She moved quickly to hold the horse's bridle as an open MGB roared up from the direction of the main entrance. It braked beside the CID car, then the driver, seeing Martin talking to Ruth, swung into the stable yard and stopped beside them.

"What is it you want? We don't encourage visitors here, you know."

Martin did not react to the insulting tone of the young man's voice. He was in his early twenties and evidently had the highest possible opinion of himself. He wore a roll-neck sweater and a check cap. His eyes were arrogant and there was the suggestion of a permanent sneer about the set of his mouth.

"I'm here to talk to Colonel Reams," Martin said.

The young man's eyes ran over the Inspector's person, somehow managing to imply that his neat hat, overcoat and well-polished shoes were indications of some inferior breed.

"If you're selling anything — you're wasting your time."

"I'm not selling anything." Martin's manner was still unruffled. "And I rather doubt whether I'm wasting my time."

A flicker of doubt showed in the other man's face. He switched his attention to Ruth. His tone of voice changed to one of familiarity.

"I've found the key to the Land-Rover."

He put his hand onto the passenger's seat, picked up a key-ring and flung it towards her. It fell short, but he was already ramming the gear-lever into first. The horse reared its head up and Ruth had her hands full as the MG, its wheels spinning, accelerated away. Martin picked the key-ring up. As it lay in his palm he saw that it bore the familiar emblem of Cavalier Toys.

"Charming young man. Lord Kingsdown himself, I presume?" He handed her the key on its ring. Ruth took it, still glaring at the disappearing sports-car.

"That's Tom Reams. The only blot on the horizon so far as I'm concerned."

"Tom Reams . . . Colonel Reams' son?"

"Nephew," she said shortly. "I've almost left on two occasions because of him. But the Colonel persuaded me to stay on.

"I see. And what does Mr. Tom Reams do, exactly?"

She had begun to lead the horse towards the paddock. Martin fell into step beside her.

"That's a good question. He's supposed to be Colonel Reams' assistant but he spends most of his time selling second-hand cars. He's even trying to sell me one." She laughed and then turned to look at him enquiringly. "What is it you want to see the Colonel about, Martin?"

"I'm making enquiries about a girl called Judy Clayton. She was murdered."

Ruth halted. The horse champed on its bit, impatient to move on. "Judy Clayton? Oh, yes — yes, I read about it."

"I wondered if, by any chance, she'd been here, to the stables?"

She hesitated fractionally before answering rather rapidly. "No, I — don't think so. Not to my knowledge."

It was the horse who gave her the excuse to avoid any further questions. It was beating a tattoo with its hind legs and tossing its head, forcing her to grip the reins tightly.

"Martin, if you'll excuse me, I've got half a dozen horses to exercise."

"Yes, of course. Nice to see you again, Ruth."

He watched her as she put a foot in the stirrup and then swung the other leg over the saddle in a lithe, fluid movement.

"Give my love to Sue if you see her," she said, looking down at him.

"Yes. Yes, I will," Martin said, without much hope that he would ever deliver the message. "Look, the Sergeant and I will probably be having a bite to eat at The Golden Swan. Why don't you join us?"

"I'd like to but — not this morning, I'm afraid."

"Well, another time, perhaps?"

"Yes, I'd love to. Goodbye, Martin." She pulled on a rein to swing the horse round, then both rider and mount presented their back view to him.

"Goodbye, Ruth," Martin said, watching the trim figure with a touch of wistfulness.

He was thankful that there was no sign of the MGB outside

the building which Ruth had indicated. A Volvo Estate car drawn up in front of the door led him to hope that the Colonel was in his office. Leaving Kennedy to get what joy he could from the fast receding figure of Ruth Jensen he went through an empty outer office and knocked on the only door opening off it.

"Come!" a strong voice shouted from inside.

Martin walked in and found himself in a surprisingly efficient-looking room with modern furniture and office equipment. One whole wall was occupied by a bank of filing cabinets, presumably containing records of the horses trained by the Colonel. Every square foot of available wall space was covered with framed photos of past race winners, many of them being led into the winners' enclosure by delighted owners in grey top-hats and tail-coats.

The Colonel was about forty-five with an alert, almost ruthless face. He had a carefully-trimmed moustache and neat hair. He wore a newish hacking jacket in bold check. The eyes which looked up to inspect his visitor were those of an army officer.

"Colonel Reams?"

"Yes," the Colonel confirmed, his manner doing nothing to make things easier for a visitor.

"My name is Denson, sir. Detective-Inspector Denson. Could you spare me a few moments, sir?"

At mention of a rank in the Force, Reams pushed his chair back and stood up.

"Why, yes, of course. Sit down, Inspector." He indicated one of the easy-chairs and sat down in the other himself. "What can I do for you?"

"I'm investigating a murder case, sir. A girl called Judy Clayton was murdered and we . . ."

"Yes, I know," Reams interrupted, nodding. "I read about it. The chap who did it committed suicide, is that right?"

He spoke as if assuming that the case must now be closed. Martin took a photograph out of his pocket.

"There are still one or two loose ends to be tied up, sir." He handed Reams the photo. "This is a photograph of Miss Clayton."

The Colonel gave the photograph a brief scrutiny and then looked up.

"Well?"

"Did you ever meet her, sir?"

"Me?" Reams smiled at such an apparently ridiculous suggestion. "Good heavens, no! What makes you think I might have done?"

"I wondered if she was friendly with someone here, at the stables?"

"Not to my knowledge." Reams shook his head and handed the photograph back to Martin.

"Would you have known about it, if she had been?"

"Yes, I think so," Reams said confidently. "We don't just let people drop in when they feel like it."

"No, I don't imagine you do, sir."

As so often, Martin's quiet and polite remarks, combined with the placid but somehow sceptical expression of his blue eyes, provoked a reaction.

"Look, Inspector, what's this all about? Why are you asking me these questions?"

"During the past six months Miss Clayton made a great deal of money out of horse racing — she actually backed five winners in a row."

"Smart girl," Reams commented drily.

"It just so happens that the horses in question were trained by you, Colonel."

"That makes her even smarter." Reams recrossed his legs. "My dear Inspector, if all the people who back my horses were friendly with someone or other in my stables then, believe you me, we'd have a lot of friends." He favoured Martin with a bland smile.

"Yes, I imagine you would, sir. But it wasn't just the fact that she backed the horses that brought me here."

"No?" Reams said, but he managed to look as if he was not particularly interested in the answer.

"On the day she was murdered she accepted a lift in a car. David Walker's car."

"The chap who committed suicide?"

"Yes. He picked her up near a pub called The Golden Swan."

"The Golden Swan? That's just down the road."

"Yes, I know, sir."

Reams was frowning with concentration, very much the man who wants nothing more than to assist the police in their enquiries. "I'm beginning to see what you're getting at. You think she might have been here, to see someone, the day she was murdered?"

"Yes."

"Well, I must confess I didn't see her." Reams' eyes patrolled the rows of photographs on the wall behind Martin. "I can't ever remember seeing her around."

"It was just a thought, sir. A vague idea of mine." Martin stood up and held out his hand. "I won't take up any more of your time."

Reams opened the office door for him and waited politely till he had gone through the outer room. As he saw the Inspector coming Kennedy started the engine.

"What's he like?" he asked, as Martin slid into the passenger's seat.

Martin reached up to pull the safety-belt across his chest. "I shouldn't think he backs many losers."

The Golden Swan was a more pretentious place than The Grapevine. Its position on a crossroads and fronting onto a main road brought a steady trade from motorists. There were two bars and a separate dining-room staffed by foreign waiters. It was just coming up to lunch-time when the police officers drew into the car park. Martin was still hoping that Ruth Jensen would change her mind and join them for lunch.

"These are on me," Kennedy said as they entered the lounge bar. "What'll it be?"

"A tomato juice, Harry. With a spot of Worcester sauce."

"Right. You grab that table while I get the drinks."

Martin amused himself by watching the customers till Kennedy came towards him with a small glass of tomato juice in one hand and a pint of beer in the other.

"I take it I'm driving this afternoon." Martin nodded at the tankard as he moved over to make room for the Sergeant's large form.

"The car's booked out in your name." Kennedy took a long pull at his beer. "The dining-room's pretty crowded, by the way; maybe we'd better reserve a table."

"Knowing how irritable you get when you miss lunch, I've just done it."

The two men had switched their minds away from the investigation, a form of relaxation which was necessary during these tough cases which could go on for weeks. They discussed their respective holiday plans and were moving on to the costs of running a car nowadays when a girl wearing a waitress's apron came up to their table.

"Excuse me, are you Inspector Denson, sir?"

"Yes, I am," Martin replied, wondering how she had been able to pick him out amongst all the other customers.

"You're wanted on the telephone."

"Oh, thank you." Martin finished off his tomato juice. "Where is it?"

"In the hall, sir."

There was a telephone cubicle in the hall alongside the hotel's reception desk. The receptionist indicaied that she had switched the call through to there. Martin closed the door and picked up the receiver.

"Denson speaking."

"Martin? This is Ruth Jensen."

"Why, hello, Ruth."

"Martin, there's something I ought to have told you this morning," she said quickly. "I meant to tell you, but — I didn't want to get Colonel Reams into trouble

"Is it about Judy Clayton?"

"Yes." She paused, and when she went on the sentences came out jerkily. "I saw her, the day she was murdered. She came to the stables . . . She was with Tom Reams . . ."

Ruth's voice had faded, as if she had turned her face away from the 'phone to look round.

71

"Go on, Ruth."

"I was in the office building looking for something and Tom's
car drove into the paddock. It stopped outside the window and I
could hear what they were saying. They were talking about .."
"About what? Can you speak up? We've got a bad line." "About
the man that . . . committed suicide."

"David Walker?" Martin, who was always conscious that
telephone conversations are the easiest to overhear, kept his
voice down, despite his surprise.

"Yes. Tom said he'd heard that David Walker's wife . . . Look,
Martin, it's difficult to talk in a call-box. I think we'd better arrange to meet somewhere."

Martin frowned in annoyance as the sound of pips warned
that Ruth had used up her time. She must have had fresh coins
ready for after a few seconds he heard her voice again.

"What time do you finish work?" he asked.

"About six. I can meet you this evening if you like, in Guildfleet."

"I can easily drive down here again if you'd like me to."

"No, no," she said quickly. "I'd sooner come to Guildfleet, if
you don't mind."

"All right, let's meet at my place. Number four, Leonard
Close. It's a mews next to Marshalls the stationers. I'm on the
second floor."

"I'll be there about eight o'clock."

"Right. See you then."

Martin heard the click at the other end before he put his own
receiver down. He stood for a moment, wondering why the conversation had made him feel so uneasy. Then, becoming conscious
of the smell of stale cigarette smoke mingled with some kind of
disinfectant spray, he pushed open the door of the booth.

The three-course set luncheon was such a good buy that the
two men settled down to really enjoy their lunch. They had been
in the dining-room for an hour and a half when Martin paid the
bill.

Kennedy checked his watch as they crossed the car park.

"Twenty to three. We should be in Guildfleet by half past —"
Martin nodded and went round to the door on the driver's side.

Kennedy pushed the passenger's seat back, stretched his legs
and folded his arms as Martin took the car out onto the road back
to Guildfleet. He thought that his Sergeant was settling down for
a nice sleep and was surprised when Kennedy spoke. Evidently he
had been mulling over the Inspector's account of his conversation
with Ruth Jensen.

"You say she sounded worried?"

"Not just worried — tense. Almost frightened, in fact." "How
long have you known her?"

"About four or five years. She's a great friend of Sue's. She and
her husband often used to come to the cottage."

He pulled out to pass a long vehicle which was travelling at a
good forty miles an hour. The driver flashed his lights, giving the
standard signal that the passing vehicle was clear. Martin raised a
hand in acknowledgment.

"Whichever way you look at it, there's something damn funny
about this case, Harry. Every time we make enquiries, every time
something happens, we find ourselves back in square one."

"Square one being?"

"That David Walker knew Judy Clayton, picked her up by ar-
rangement, killed her, and then conveniently committed suicide."

"And you don't think that's what happened?"

Martin took his eyes off the road for long enough to glance at
Kennedy. "No, I don't."

Kennedy grunted and did not pursue the question further. A
minute or two later his head dropped forward, jerked up and then
dropped again. Martin smiled to himself. He did not grudge Kennedy his cat-nap. Unless he was very much mistaken the young
man was going to be doing a good deal of overtime before this
case was broken.

A few miles further on he noticed that the brake lights of the
car he was following had flashed just before it disappeared round
the bend ahead. He slowed and took the corner warily, but even at
reduced speed he had to brake hard to avoid ramming the rear of

the car in front. Kennedy was jerked forward against his seat-belt. He shook his head and opened his eyes.

A hundred yards ahead an articulated lorry was slewed sideways, almost completely blocking the road. Beyond it was the white shape of an ambulance. It had evidently just arrived, for the crew were dismounting and running towards the small group which had formed round something which was still invisible. Two police cars were already on the scene, their blue lights flashing.

Martin switched off his engine and got out. As he walked past the line of stationary vehicles, Kennedy was going back to wave down traffic coming round the bend. Martin saw now that one of the police officers was talking to the driver of the lorry, who was standing beside his vehicle, miserably smoking a cigarette. As he came abreast of the lorry he saw the upturned wheels of a capsised sports car. The black rubber marks and the churned up rurf at the verge told all too plainly what had happened. Near the car a human form had been completely covered by a rug. The ambulance men were trying to extricate someone else from the wreckage.

The policeman standing beside the driver was about to tell Martin to keep back when he recognised the Inspector.

"Good afternoon, sir." He saluted and Martin nodded acknowledgment. "It shouldn't be long now. They're just getting the passenger out, then we can get the lorry away and let you through."

"It looks pretty serious," Martin said.

"The driver — a young chap called Tom Reams — was killed." He gestured towards the still form under the blanket. "And I must say, he bought it! Driving like a maniac. We don't know about the passenger yet."

Martin's interest had sharpened at mention of Tom Reams. He went towards the group surrounding the wrecked car and pushed his way between the half-dozen bystanders who were watching the ambulance men. They had got the second victim out of the car and onto a stretcher. It was a woman. Martin just had time to recoognise the features of Ruth Jensen before one of the ambulance men closed her eyes and pulled the sheet over her face.

He watched in shocked disbelief as the stretcher was lifted and carried towards the ambulance. He just could not believe that the mangled and disfigured form was that of the girl he had seen swing herself onto the back of a horse only a few hours ago.

He was still standing on the same spot when Harry Kennedy came excitedly towards him, pushing a way through the hushed and awed little crowd.

"It's Tom Reams' car! Is he —?"

He stopped, following the direction of Martin's eyes. The ambulance men had returned for the second body. Kennedy waited till they had put the blanketed form onto a stretcher and started back towards the ambulance.

"He's dead?"

"They both are."

"Both?" repeated Kennedy, who had not seen the first stretcher.

"Ruth Jensen was with him," Martin said very quietly.

The lorry driver was just lighting yet another cigarette when Martin came over to talk to him. His hands were trembling and he looked in need of some medical attention himself.

"What happened?" Martin asked.

"Who are you?" the driver demanded, seeking relief from his shock in belligerence.

"Detective-Inspector Denson." As he saw the man's face register alarm he added quickly: "The lady in the car was a friend of mine."

"A friend of yours! Oh, my God! I'm sorry, mate." The driver shook his head and sucked air through his teeth. "But I just hadn't a chance! He was driving like a flaming madman — wasn't even looking where he was going. He was looking at the bird the whole time. There was nothing I could do! Honest, guy! Couldn't do a ruddy thing."

Martin had stopped listening to the man's protestations. The ambulance had started up. The little group had to step back to give it room to turn. It moved off up the road without urgency, its blue light switched off. The police officers had got out their

75

measuring tapes and were making notes on the scene of the accident, but Martin still stood there with his hat off, watching the white vehicle till it vanished round a bend.

"I knew he'd come a cropper sooner or later," Colonel Reams said. "He used to drive like a maniac. God knows, I warned him often enough! But it was no use at all, he just didn't want to know."

The Colonel had taken the news with only a slight stiffening of his features. The early return of the police officers and something about their manner had warned him to prepare himself. When Martin had finished the stark announcement he turned away and stood looking out of the window of his office towards the paddock, where half a dozen horses were grazing.

Now he turned and came back into the middle of the room.

"As for Ruth . . . It's tragic. It really is! You couldn't have met a nicer girl . . ."

"I know," Martin interposed. "She was a friend of my wife's."

"I didn't realise that." Colonel Reams contemplated Martin with faint surprise.

"We used to see quite a lot of her at one time."

Reams gestured towards the chairs and they all sat down. "Was Mrs. Jensen very friendly with your nephew, sir?" Kennedy asked.

Reams was caught slightly off balance by this question coming from a new quarter.

"No, they weren't at all friendly. That's what I don't understand. What was Ruth doing in the car? I just can't imagine her accepting a lift from Tom." He was shaking his head in bewilderment as he took a cigarette from a gold case and put it in his mouth.

"Did Tom say where he was going when he left here?" Martin asked.

"No. I assumed he was going into the village for lunch. But Ruth didn't go with him, I'm sure of that."

"When was the last time you saw Ruth?"

Reams snapped his lighter and put the flame to his cigarette. "I saw her just before lunch, about a quarter to one. She appeared to be going for a stroll."

"Did she say she was going for a walk?"

"No," Reams said, slightly resentful at Martin's questioning his opinion. "But she frequently did at lunchtime. My God, Ruth!" He ran his hand through his hair in a slightly theatrical gesture. "I still can't believe it! I just can't believe it, Inspector!"

Martin gave him a few moments before he sprung his next question.

"How far is the nearest 'phone box from here?"

"The nearest 'phone box?" Reams repeated, puzzled by the question. "It's about a mile and a half down the road."

"Was she walking in that direction?"

"Yes, but . . ." The Colonel pointed to the telephone on his desk. "If she'd wanted to telephone anyone she'd have used this. She frequently did."

"But not this morning, Colonel," Martin told him quietly.

"What do you mean?" There was a slight edge in Reams voice. Why didn't the fellow come out with it, instead of making mysterious innuendoes?

"The Sergeant and I had lunch in the village. While we were having a drink Ruth telephoned me from a call-box. I suspect the one down the road. It was about ten past one so that ties up with what you've just told us."

"But why should she use a . . ." Reams stopped and gave Martin a long, thoughtful look. "It's none of my business, but — what did she telephone you about, Inspector?"

"About Judy Clayton," Martin answered without hesitation. "She said she'd seen the girl — here, at the stables, talking to your nephew."

"Oh. Oh, I see." Reams thoughtfully extinguished his cigarette in the ash-tray. "I take it you'd previously questioned her about Miss Clayton?"

"Yes, and for some reason or other she'd lied to me."

Reams leaned across to replace the ash-tray on his desk. He

reflected for a few seconds and then gave Martin a direct look. "I think perhaps I can explain that, Inspector."

"Then I wish you would, sir."

A man of action all his life, Colonel Reams felt ill at ease sitting down for a conversation of this kind, especially when it was the other person who was calling the tune.

"Do you mind if we stroll down to the stables?" he asked Martin, getting to his feet. "With Ruth gone I'll have to arrange for one of my lads to exercise her horses."

Martin was as fond of fresh air as anyone and agreed at once. His suspicion that Reams was trying to avoid further revelations was dispelled as soon as they were outside. The Colonel picked up the thread of the conversation where they had broken it off.

"To answer your question, Inspector, I think Ruth was covering up."

"Covering up?"

"Yes. For me."

"You mean, you knew your nephew had seen Miss Clayton. You knew he was friendly with her?"

"Yes . . ." Reams was looking away towards the field where a stable lad was putting a bridle on one of the horses that had been grazing.

"Why didn't you tell me that, this morning?"

"What was the point? I just didn't see any sense in getting my nephew involved in a murder case when you already knew who had committed the murder."

"You should have let me be the judge of that, sir."

"Yes, I'm sorry, Inspector." The mild reproof in Martin's voice had left Reams unmoved. He added with formality: "I apologise."

"Now perhaps you'll tell me the truth?"

"There isn't a great deal to tell. Tom brought Judy Clayton here, to the stables, on two occasions. I took an instant dislike to the girl and told Tom not to have anything more to do with her. You can imagine his reaction."

The sound of hooves from behind made Reams turn. They all drew back as a string of race horses, ridden by three lads and a young girl in jeans, trotted past. Reams watched the movement of the animals critically as they went by towards the stable yard.

"Go on, sir," Martin prompted, as they walked on again.

"I knew he was still seeing her, of course — although he didn't have the nerve to bring her back here, thank God! Then one morning — it was the day she was murdered — I saw the two of them in the village."

From the other side of Reams Kennedy's head turned in surprise. "What time was that?" the Sergeant asked.

"It was fairly early, about half-past eight, I should imagine."

"So what did you do about it?" Martin asked.

"Later in the day I told Tom I'd seen them and he said I needn't lose any sleep over it because he'd finished with her." "You mean — he'd broken things off?"

"Yes. That's exactly what I mean."

"Did he tell you why he'd broken things off?" Martin persisted, ignoring the Colonel's irritation.

"Yes. He said she was having an affair with someone else. Someone in Guildfleet. I imagine he was referring to the chap who committed suicide — David . . . what was his name?"

"David Walker. Yes, I imagine he was, sir." They were approaching the stable yard. The lads were dismounting and starting to remove the saddles from the horses. "Is there anything else you'd like to tell me, sir, before I leave? Anything you might, perhaps, have inadvertently forgotten?"

"No, except that . . ." Reams stopped and faced Martin. "I'm very sorry about this morning. I was a damn fool. I should have told you the truth."

"Yes, I think you should have done," Martin agreed, his face serious.

Martin was silent as the two officers walked back to their own car, and Kennedy was puzzling over this new and unexpected turn. Neither of them spoke till they had opened the doors and were settling into their seats.

"Well," Kennedy observed, "we're back again where we started — with David Walker."

"Yes. It looks like it. Someone's determined to keep us in square one, Harry."

The working day had ended and the employees were streaming out of the Cavalier Toys factory as Martin drove in through the gates. He had returned the CID car and Sergeant Kennedy to the police station and was driving his own vehicle.

It was easy to find a free space in the car park which was rapidly emptying. He positioned himself so that he could watch the gates and the entrance to the office block. For a few moments he watched the scene with amusement. The work-force was evacuating the premises with as much urgency as if it had been on fire. In cars, motor-cycles, bicycles and on foot they were streaming out into the main road, forcing passing traffic to stop and give them priority. Martin wondered how some of them would react to the hours a policeman is expected to work.

A man and woman emerging from the office block drew his attention. The man was holding the woman's arm and they were so deeply absorbed in their conversation that they did not even acknowledge the salute from the uniformed commissionaire at the entrance. They got into a Jaguar and joined the line of vehicles waiting to pass through the gates.

Martin picked up an evening paper and began to glance through the headlines, keeping an eye on the office block entrance. About ten minutes later Arthur Eastwood came out of the door. He looked flustered and unhappy as he covered the short distance to the specially reserved space where his car stood waiting, not even responding to the greetings of a couple of the clerical staff who passed. He started the Rover, which was facing outwards, and Martin knew that he would be bound to come past him on his way to the gates.

He made no attempt at concealing his face nor any move to attract Eastwood's attention. The Rover was almost abreast of Martin's car when Eastwood glanced across, saw the Inspector watching him and braked sharply to a halt. He lowered his window.

"Hello, Inspector! Can I help you?"

"No, thank you, sir. I'm waiting for my wife."

"Oh." Arthur tried not to show his surprise. "Well, she shouldn't be very long."

"Was that Mrs. Walker I saw just now, with Mr. Norton?"

"It was," Arthur said and at once the cause of his discomfiture was evident. "It was indeed! Incidentally, Inspector, did you know that, quite apart from running a driving school, Mr. Norton's a financier?"

"No, I'm afraid I didn't."

"Well, apparently he is," Arthur said with irritation. "According to Eve — Mrs. Walker, he's the Charlie Clore of Guildfleet."

Martin smiled. "I find that difficult to believe, sir."

"Yes, so do I." Arthur nodded emphatic agreement and began to wind his window up. "Good night, Inspector."

"Good night, sir."

Martin had to wait another five minutes before he saw Sue coming out. She smiled at the commissionaire and thoughtfully descended the steps. She looked particularly attractive in a lemon-coloured suit with a gay scarf tied with careless artistry round her neck. As she began to walk towards the entrance, by now almost clear of vehicles, Martin got out of his car and began to move towards her on a converging line. He was only a few paces from her when she looked up and saw him. Martin stopped.

"Hello, Sue," he said quietly.

"Martin!" She halted in her tracks. "What are you doing here?"

"Waiting for you."

As always now he saw her race harden and her eyes grow remote. "Martin, I'm sorry," she said tightly. "I've got an appointment this evening . . ."

"Sue, get in the car. I've got something I want to tell you."

"Martin, I've told you!" she said with weary exasperation. "I keep on telling you! It's just no use your trying to persuade me to . . ."

"Sue, listen to me!" said Martin with abrupt authority. "I want to talk to you about Ruth Jensen." He paused. He had wanted to break this to her more gently but she was giving him no chance. "She's dead. She was killed in a road accident this afternoon."

"Oh, no! Not Ruth!"

Sue's hand went to her mouth and her eyes widened in shock. Martin took a step forward, put his fingers round her arm and led her towards his car.

"Sue, please get in," he said gently, opening the passenger door for her. "I've got to talk to you."

For once she let herself be persuaded. She was groping for a handkerchief as he leaned across her to fasten the passenger's safety-belt.

Half an hour later Sue was sitting at one end of the settee in Martin's flat, a glass of almost neat whisky in her hands. She had taken off her shoes and had her legs rucked under her. The books and records which usually occupied the settee had been dumped on the floor.

In her distress she had not questioned Martin's suggestion to bring her back to his flat and give her a good strong drink. Now she was beginning to recover from the shock of his announcement, thanks to the drink and, though she would not admit it to herself, the concern Martin had shown for her feelings.

He had made no attempt to sit down himself and at the moment was behind her at the table where he kept his small supply of drinks. As it was past six, he allowed himself a little gin with the tonic he was pouring.

"Oh no. No doubt about the accident," he was saying. "It was genuine all right. But the thing that puzzles me is — what was Ruth doing in the car? Unless, of course, Tom was trying to sell it to her."

Sue's fingers played with the brooch she was wearing on a chain round her neck. "Is that likely?"

"It's a possibility. She said something about him dealing in second-hand cars." He came round in front of the settee, taking one of the Cavalier key-rings from his pocket. "Sue, how many of your friends have got key-rings like this?"

Sue scarcely glanced at the ring. "Oh, practically everyone at the factory's got one."

"They're not difficult to come by?"

"Good heavens, no! At Christmas we must have given dozens of them away."

"When you say 'we' . . ."

"I mean Mr. Eastwood. He usually distributes them."

"Mr. Eastwood, himself?"

"Yes. He loves to do that sort of thing. At the end of the year we usually get a bonus, and he always hands out the cheque himself."

"I see."

Martin picked up her jacket, which she had thrown on the arm of the settee and put it carefully over the back of a chair. "But why are you interested in the key-rings?"

"Judy Clayton had one — and so has Colonel Reams." He held the key-ring between finger and thumb, studying it as if it could tell him something. "Tell me, had you heard of Colonel Reams before I mentioned him?"

She hesitated, shaking her head slowly. "No, I . . .don't think so."

"No one's ever mentioned his name at the office?"

"Not that I . . ." Sue put her feet to the floor and sat up straight. "Wait a minute! I have a feeling Mr. Eastwood had a letter from someone called Reams."

"When?"

"About six months ago, I should say."

"What was the letter about — can you remember?"

She dropped her eyes and tapped the front of her forehead to jog her memory. "No, I'm afraid I can't. All I remember is that it certainly annoyed the old boy."

"Could you get hold of the letter?"

"Well . . . I think so. It's probably on the file."

"I'd be grateful if you would."

"All right," she said, and smiled at him for the first time. "I'll see what I can do."

"Can I fill your glass up?"

She shook her head and handed him the empty glass. As he

took it to the drinks table she really looked at the room for the first time. The place needed a thoroughly good tidying up. He ought to get a set of shelves for all those books and a cabinet for the records. The bureau looked terribly out of place stuck in the corner like that, and as for the dust —!

"Sue, about David Walker," Martin cut in on her thoughts. "What sort of chap was he? Did you like him?"

"Yes, I did. He was a hard worker; a hard task-master at times, but I liked him."

"Were you surprised when you heard that he'd been having an affair with Judy Clayton?"

"Very surprised, and I don't believe it." She slipped her feet into her shoes and stood up. She was recovering from the moment of weakness now, beginning to regret that she'd agreed to come back to his flat.

"Why don't you?"

"I don't believe he was friendly with her. I don't even believe he knew the girl."

"Then why did he kill her?"

"I don't think he did kill her. I agree with Mr. Eastwood. I don't think he committed the murder and I certainly don't think he committed suicide."

"Then what happened?"

"I — I just can't imagine." Sue shrugged, turned away towards the window. It was her first experience of Martin in action on a criminal investigation and she was seeing a completely new side of him. It was a strange, slightly exciting experience to be inter-rogated like this by a man you had lived with for years. She was well aware that just at the moment she was nothing more to him than a witness who might provide useful information. "I sup-pose . . .someone must have murdered both of them."

"Tell me more about him, Sue."

"What is it you want to know?" Her face had a hint of the old mischief in it. "Whether he made a pass at me?"

"Did he?"

"No, he didn't."

"Did he notice you?"

"It depends what you mean by notice . . ."

"You know what I mean by notice."

She stared at him defiantly, her fingers again playing with the brooch at her bosom.

"Yes, he noticed me."

"Did you ever have a meal with him, or a drink perhaps?"

She had begun a tour of the small room, briefly touching objects she remembered from their old home.

"He took me to The Crown just before Christmas. We had a drink together."

"What did you talk about?"

"His wife."

The answer had evidently surprised Martin. He moved round so that he could see her face better.

"His wife?"

"Yes, he was crazy about her." Something about the way she said the words told Martin that Sue's opinion of Evelyn Walker was not high.

"Sue, I accept what you've told me about Walker, about the fact that you liked him. But isn't it possible that you were mistaken and that outside the office he was quite a different person?"

"Yes, it's possible, but — I don't think he was."

"And what about Mrs. Walker?"

"What about her?"

"Have you met her?"

"Yes."

"Do you like her?"

"No."

"Why not?"

"I don't know why, I always have the feeling that . . .she's not quite what she seems to be."

"What does that mean, exactly?"

"A lot of people I know think she's stupid, that she's only interested in having a good time. I . . .think there's more to her than that."

"Yes, I know what you mean."

Sue took her coat from the back of the chair and slipped it on. "Look, I'm sorry, I must be making a move. I've got an appointment this evening."

Martin bit off his question just in time. He had been on the verge of asking her who she was supposed to be meeting.

"You won't forget about that letter?"

"No." Half way to the door she paused, fingering the brooch. "Reams . . . I wonder if I'm right about the name?"

"I'd be grateful if you'd check."

He was escorting her through the hall when the brooch suddenly detached itself from the chain. Sue tried to grab it as it slid down her front. Martin, stooping with a swift reflex action, caught it just before it hit the floor.

"I see you're still having the same old trouble." He smiled as he handed the brooch back to her.

"Yes." She turned it over to look at the clasp. "I keep meaning to take it in to be repaired, but somehow I never seem to get round to it."

The trivial incident had set up some strange current between them. They stood there awkwardly for a moment, neither of them able to find the right words to part on.

Sue started as the door bell rang with sudden stridence.

"That's probably Harry Kennedy," Martin said, moving to twist the Yale knob. "They've invited me out to dinner and he's picking me up."

Martin managed to conceal his surprise when he opened the door and saw who his visitor was. Andy Mason's finger was still on the bell-push. The alacrity with which the door had been opened had startled him and as he saw Sue Denson standing in the hall his expression became even more embarrassed.

"Hello, Mr. Mason!" Martin exclaimed.

"I'm sorry to disturb you, Inspector, but . . ." He pretended to see Sue for the first time. "Oh, good evening, Miss — er — Mrs . . ."

"Good evening," Sue replied with a faint smile of amusement.

"Come along in, Mr. Mason." Martin stood back, holding the

door wide and turned to Sue. "I'll 'phone you. Probably tomorrow afternoon."

"All right." She hesitated, then added: "But make it late — not before five-thirty."

"I'll remember that."

Martin closed the door on her and then gave his attention to Andy Mason. "What can I do for you, Mr. Mason?"

"I'm sorry, dropping in on you like this. I should have telephoned your office and made an appointment."

"That's all right, don't worry about that. Come on in."

A faint reminder of Sue's perfume still lingered in the sitting-room as Martin showed his guest in.

"Would you care for a drink?" Martin suggested, anxious to put the other man at his ease.

"Er — no, I won't have one, not at the moment. Thank you very much."

Martin waved a hand towards the settee. "Sit down."

Andy sat down gingerly on the settee, perching himself on the edge in an awkward fashion.

"Look, Inspector, I'll come straight to the point. I want to talk to you about my sister — Mrs. Walker. I'm worried about her and I don't quite know what to do. I'd be very grateful if you'd . . .give me your advice."

"If I can help you, Mr. Mason, I will — certainly."

Martin pulled up an upright chair, removed a couple of books and sat down at a slight angle to the settee.

"My sister's having an affair with a man called Roy Norton, you probably know that. If you don't, you're about the only man in Guildfleet who doesn't."

Martin nodded confirmation and waited for him to go on.

"Well, this afternoon I had a 'phone call from Arthur Eastwood. To say he was angry would be the under-statement of the year. He was livid! Apparently, Evelyn — my sister — had an appointment to see him this afternoon and — well, she took Roy Norton along with her."

Andy removed his spectacles and began to polish them with

his handkerchief, the muscles round his eyes contracting with the effort to focus.

"Go on," Martin prompted.

"According to Arthur, Norton started asking a lot of damn silly questions about the business; shooting his mouth off, pretending he was the financial genius of all time. In the end Arthur lost his temper and threatened to throw him out of the office."

He replaced his spectacles and glanced at Martin to see how he was reacting to this recital.

"Yes, I can imagine he would." Martin could not help feeling that Andy's statement had been rehearsed. "But tell me, what is it you want me to do, Mr. Mason?"

"I don't know that you can do anything, Inspector." Andy shook his head hopelessly. "It's just that I thought . . .my sister's an extremely wealthy woman, at least she will be when probate's granted. Roy Norton knows this and he's taking advantage of her."

"Well, I'm sorry, Mr. Mason, I can't help you. This is purely a family matter."

"I thought perhaps if you had a word with her . . ."

"She'll probably tell me to take a running jump, or get lost." Martin smiled. "And quite frankly I wouldn't blame her."

"Well, what am I going to do? Just stand by and let Norton take over?"

Martin had no intention of answering Andy's rhetorical question. He hoped Andy would soon get round to the real purpose of his visit.

"Have you spoken to your sister?"

"Yes, I've just left her."

"And what happened?"

"What I knew would happen. She told me to mind my own damn business." Andy forced a short laugh. "Which is a bit rich, when you consider it's not so long ago that both she and David talked me into putting some money into Cavalier Toys. Good God, I ask you — fancy having money in a firm run by Roy Norton!"

Andy's indignation sounded a little false to Martin's ears.

"I hardly think Mr. Norton will be allowed to run this firm, Mr. Mason. But tell me: is this the only reason you wanted to see me?"

"No , I . . ." Andy leaned back on the cushions, crossed his legs and flicked a small spot of dust off his trouser leg. "There was something else, Inspector."

"I rather thought there might be."

"I don't know whether you're aware of the fact or not, but certain people — and I must confess I'm one of them — are not too happy about the note David was supposed to have left for Arthur Eastwood."

"You don't think Mr. Walker typed the note?"

"No, I don't." Andy was talking more easily and plausibly now. "And neither does Arthur. In the first place David would never have written a note like that, and in the second place . . ."

"Go on."

"Well, in the second place I just don't believe that David did commit suicide."

"Then what do you think happened?"

"I think he was murdered." Andy managed to look at Martin directly as he said this. Martin held his eyes for a second. "There's usually a motive for murder."

"There's usually a motive for suicide."

"Surely it was in the letter. Blackmail."

"I don't accept that." Andy shook his head, leaned forward and clasped his fingers. "David was a very determined character. Even if he was having an affair with anyone, which I don't believe, he'd never allow himself to be blackmailed."

"All right, let's suppose for a moment it murder. Who killed him? And what was the motive?"

Andy did not answer for a long time. He stared at the carpet and seemed to be working something out in his mind. At last he looked up.

"I don't want to throw suspicion onto anyone, that's the last thing I want to do, but . . . There's a girl called Doreen Summers

— she's a waitress — she works at The Bear in Guildfleet. Her brother, Norman, is employed by me at The Grapevine."

"Oh, yes?"

"Well, the night that David was shot, my sister and Roy Norton had dinner at The Bear. Apparently they go there quite often. According to Norman, Doreen was on duty that evening and she served them."

Andy was feeding Martin the information in penny packets, waiting for him to digest each morsel before he produced the next tit-bit.

"Go on, Mr. Mason," Martin said, with some impatience.

"At about eight o'clock, just as Doreen was about to serve coffee, Roy Norton suddenly got up from the table and left the hotel. He returned about half an hour later."

"Have you any idea where he went?"

"Well, I talked to Evelyn about it and she said he had to make an important telephone call so he went back to his office."

"Why didn't he make it from the hotel?"

"Exactly — that's what I said. Apparently he had some papers at the office that he wanted to refer to."

"I see. This was at eight o'clock?"

"Yes, so I understand," Andy confirmed. He added musingly: "It takes me about twelve minutes to walk from The Bear to my sister's house."

"You're a slow walker, Mr. Mason. I've done it in eight." The door bell had rung out in the hall. Martin stood up to make it plain to his visitor that the interview was at an end. "Now, if you'll excuse me, sir . . ."

Andy uncoiled his long body and got to his feet.

"Yes, of course. I'm sorry to have troubled you, Inspector. But — well, you can understand why I'm worried. About my sister, I mean."

"I can indeed, sir." Martin put a hand out to shepherd Andy into the hall. He went past him to open the door. "Hello, Harry! Come in!"

Kennedy checked as he saw Andy Mason. "Are you ready?"

"I will be in a minute." Martin turned back to Andy. "Good night, Mr. Mason. Don't hesitate to drop in again if you hear anything which you think might interest me."

"Thank you, Inspector." Andy, relieved now that he had said what he had come to say, slipped between them. Martin closed the door on him and started back towards the living-room.

"I shan't be a minute, Harry."

"What did he want?" Kennedy jerked his head towards the closed front door.

"He wanted to tell me something." Martin gave his faint smile. "Something I already knew."

Martin repeatedly depressed the receiver cradle of his telephone as he tried in vain to get the operator's attention. His expression was one of extreme irritation. He had done exactly as Sue had asked and waited until half-past five before 'phoning her. It was now five minutes since he had asked them to put the call through. He slammed the receiver down as the door opened and a uniformed clerk came in.

"Tomkins, what the hell's happening?"

"There's no reply, sir."

"What do you mean — no reply?" Martin demanded angrily.

"There's always someone at the office until six o'clock." "I meant — there's no reply from Mrs. Denson, sir." "Who told you that?"

"The girl on the switchboard, sir."

Martin realised he was taking it out on the unfortunate clerk.

He forced himself to relax. "All right, Tomkins. Thank you."

He tried to concentrate on the typewritten report he was reading, made a few notes in the margin. But after a minute or two he threw the pencil down. It was no good. He could not concentrate. He felt terribly let down. In spite of himself he had been looking forward all day to renewing the contact with Sue. Just for a moment there in the hall when she had been leaving he'd had the feeling that she might have said something, if only Andy had not been standing there, his spectacles glinting with curiosity. He had felt her near to him then, and not only in the physical sense. The picture of her was so vivid in his mind that the sudden jar of the 'phone made him start.

He picked up the receiver. "Hello? Inspector Denson speaking . . ."

"Martin, this is Sue."

"Hello Sue!" Somehow, all his irritaation vanished as he heard her voice. "I've been trying to get hold of you!"

"I left early to do some shopping. I'm in a call-box." "What happened? Did you find out about the letter?" "Yes, I was wrong, I'm afraid. It was from a man called Breen. He runs an employment agency in St. Albans." "Oh," Martin said, deflated. "Oh, I see."

"I'm sorry, Martin, but I told you I wasn't sure."

"Yes, I know. Well — thanks anyway, Sue."

"Goodbye, Martin."

"Sue, wait a minute!"

"What is it?"

"Please don't ring off! I want to talk to you." He paused for a moment, wondering how best to put it. "I think I've sold the cottage. I had a letter from the estate agents this morning, and well — it looks like a deal."

"I see."

He thought there was a kind of sadness in her voice.

"Sue, I'm going there this evening. I've got to collect one or two things. I suppose you wouldn't like to meet me there and . . ."

"No, I wouldn't, Martin," she cut in. "It's no use. You know as well as I do it — wouldn't work. Goodbye."

She had hung up swiftly. He replaced his own instrument more slowly. It would have been easier to bear her rejection had it not been for that moment in the flat last night and the ray of hope it had caused.

Concentration on that damned report was impossible now. The only refuge from the brooding depression which he felt threatening him lay in action. He scooped the papers up and pushed his chair back. He had relocked them in the filing cabinet and was opening the cupboard where his overcoat hung when Kennedy came in with his usual air of bearing earth-shaking tidings. He was carrying a typed memo in his hand.

"We've had a report on the suicide note. It was typed on Walker's machine and there were three sets of prints on it. Curiously enough . . ."

"Tell me later, Harry," Martin interrupted tersely, slamming the door of the cupboard.

"Yes, all right."

"I'm going to the estate agents, then on to the cottage. I'll be back about seven."

"This is important," Kennedy said reprovingly. "I think you you should . . ." Martin turned towards him and what Kennedy saw in the Inspector's face made him change his mind. "Okay, I'll tell you later."

Something about Kennedy's manner warned Martin in time. He came back from the door. "No, tell me now. What is it?"

"I was under the impression," Kennedy said carefully, "that Mrs. Walker didn't know about the note — not until you told her."

"That's right. She didn't."

Kennedy shook his head in contradiction and handed Martin the fingerprint report. "Her prints are on it."

Martin managed to get to the estate agents just before they closed at six o'clock. He took away the keys of his own cottage with a promise that he would return them the next morning so that the prospective purchaser could get in to do some measuring.

His plan to visit the cottage before having his evening meal was thwarted when he was buttonholed by the organiser of the Summer Fete, who had co-opted Martin on to the Committee. The colonel insisted on the Inspector joining him for a drink at The George and Dragon while he elaborated his latest ideas for Guildfleet's annual festival. After that Martin decided he had better eat before going out to the cottage.

In the end it was getting on for nine o'clock when, driving his own car now, he cleared the outskirts of the town on one of the minor roads. The cottage where he and Sue had lived for the happiest years of his life was situated in a quiet lane about five miles from Guildfleet. During the ten minutes it took him to make the journey the light had begun to fade from an overcast sky and his side-lights were switched on as he stopped outside the isolated building.

He climbed out, closing the door gently. The place was so peaceful that he disliked making any jarring noise to disturb it. As he stood there the rooks were returning to the group of beeches just outside his property. The birds were conversing amicably among themselves, playing tumbling games in the darkening sky. The big FOR SALE sign was mounted on two stakes beside the gate. Someone had forgotten to refasten the catch. He pushed his way in, and walked up the short path to the front door. Weeds were already sprouting through the cracks in the crazy paving and the lawn was knee-high in grass. It was uncanny how quickly nature grasped that a place had been abandoned by its humans.

He hauled the bunch of keys out of his pocket, found the one which opened the front door and inserted it in the lock. As always, it scraped the floor when it opened. Over the years the hinges had dropped slightly. When he closed it the hall was almost dark. He pressed down the light switch and the naked bulb hanging from the centre of the ceiling illuminated the hall harshly, casting sharp shadows.

It was because of these shadows that he did not see the object lying on the floor till his foot knocked against it. He stooped to pick it up. The diamonds in Sue's brooch, the one which had fallen onto the ground in his flat, glittered in the electric light. He stared at it incredulously.

The door of the sitting-room was ajar and there was no light in there. Surely she could not be waiting in the darkness of one of the bedrooms upstairs? He went to the foot of the stairs.

"Sue? It's Martin. Are you upstairs?"

The short echo of his own voice mocked him. He did not want to call again. He moved towards the living-room, pushed the door open and switched on that light also. The room looked sparsely furnished without the things he had taken away for his flat. Most of the pieces which were left had been draped in old sheets and plastic covers. The curtains had been drawn across the French windows. There was a musty smell about it and a faint tang which Martin could not identify.

For some reason the remaining sofa had been turned onto its side. He went towards it to put it upright and then stopped dead. A foot wearing a woman's shoe protruded from behind it.

"Sue!" Martin cried out involuntarily and rushed forward.

She was lying in the shadow of the sofa, sprawled without dignity, her clothes pulled out of place. Her face was hidden by a cushion, but he only had to see the thick legs and the over-weight form to know that this was not Sue.

He stepped round the body and carefully lifted the cushion. Even though the features were discoloured and twisted he had no difficulty in recognising Judy Clayton's landlady. The manner of death was apparent. Christine Bodley had been strangled and about her neck was still knotted the instrument of murder. It was the green, red and white silk scarf which he had last seen on Sue.

Chapter Three

As Martin covered the dead face of Christine Bodley he heard a faint swishing noise behind him. He straightened up quickly. The curtains at the French windows were moving. As they hung right to the floor it would have been impossible to see the feet of anyone standing there.

"Whoever you are you'd better come out."

For answer the curtains ballooned and a draught of air passed through the room. He strode across and with a quick movement pulled the curtains aside. Glass lay on the floor below the pane; it had been smashed in so that the intruder could reach the key which was still on the inside of the door. He had brought out his handkerchief and was about to remove it when he raised his head, listening. A car was coming along the lane towards the cottage.

Martin pulled the curtains back and went quickly into the hall. He stood a little back from the window which looked out onto the front garden. The car was braking to a stop in front of the gate. As it came into his field of vision he saw the blue light flashing on its roof He went to the door and had it open as Kennedy, followed by two uniformed officers, came briskly through the gate.

Kennedy stopped short when he saw the Inspector and blinked with surprise.

"Martin! What the hell is going on?"

"Mrs. Bodley. She's been murdered. She's in there."

The two constables, acting on a nod from Martin, moved past and disappeared into the house.

"Mrs. Bodley?" Kennedy echoed. "But she came to the station. She wanted to see you."

"When was this?"

"Oh, a couple of hours ago."

"Did you tell her I was here?"

"I'm afraid I did. She said it was very important and she refused to talk to . . ."

Martin had been staring towards the police car. He'd seen the woman sitting in the back seat but could not be sure till she turned her head.

"What's Sue doing there?"

"That's why we're here. Sue telephoned us." He lowered his voice, like one who is about to break bad news. "Someone tried to kill her."

"When was this?"

"About an hour ago. She changed her mind about not meeting you here and . . .Wait a minute!" Kennedy put out a hand to grasp Martin's arm as he started towards the car. "She's had a hell of a shock. Now take it easy, Martin."

Martin nodded and steadied himself. As he went through the gate, Sue had opened the door and was getting out. She was pale and shaken, obviously still in a state of shock. She did not even seem surprised to see Martin there.

"Martin, what's happened?"

"Sue, are you all right?" Martin moved quickly and put out a hand to help her.

"Yes. I changed my mind about not meeting you. I thought if we could only . . ." Her lips trembled and her eyes widened as fear returned. "Someone tried to kill me."

"Who was it, Sue?" he asked very gently.

"I don't know! He was in the cottage, waiting for me. As soon as I came through the door he grabbed hold of my scarf and . . ." She broke off and put a hand over her eyes. She had begun to tremble uncontrollably. He found his arm going round her shoulder, drawing her protectively towards him.

"Don't try to talk now. You can tell me about it later."

He steered her towards his own car, and opened the passenger door. "Stay here, Sue. I'll be back in a few minutes."

She was about to duck into the car when she straightened and looked in bewilderment towards the open door of the cottage. "Martin, what's happened?"

"Judy Clayton's landlady wanted to see me. She called at the station and Kennedy told her I was here. Unfortunately I was held up and didn't get out here till about nine . . ." He stopped, wondering whether she was really listening to him, but she said impatiently: "Go on."

"Someone must have been following her. Whoever it was suddenly realised where she was going and broke into the cottage. It wasn't you he was waiting for, Sue. It was Mrs. Bodley."

Martin was glad to leave Kennedy to handle the situation at the cottage. It would be some time before the photographers, police doctor and forensic experts could be rounded up and he was worried about Sue, sitting out there in his car, still obviously suffering from the shock and her terrifying encounter with the murderer.

"I'm going to take you back home," he told her, as he slid into the driving seat.

"Where's home?"

"Well — Would you rather go back to my place or shall I take you to yours?"

"I think I'd rather get back to the flat — my own, I mean. I really do feel a bit weak at the knees."

"Okay," Martin said, turning the car in the narrow lane. "You'll have to show me exactly where it is."

He had never seen where Sue was living now and had deliberately refrained from seeming to pry into her affairs. All he knew was that she had found a flatlet at the back of a Victorian house not far from Cavalier Toys.

"Do you feel up to telling me what happened?" he asked her as the little car moved off down the lane.

"I'll try. It's all so confused in my mind."

He listened without interrupting until they were amongst the houses of Guildfleet. Then she had to break off to direct him to Somerville Avenue where her flat was. At her direction he stopped in front of a three-storey brick house, characterised by the ornamental woodwork favoured by the late Victorians.

"Sue, I'm afraid I have quite a few questions to ask you."
"You mean — now?"

"Well, I could take you up to your flat," he pointed out quietly. "Your landlord can hardly object to a visit from your husband."

She thought about that for a moment, then gave him a wary look. "All right. But I warn you, it's not very palatial and I'm not even sure I have anything to drink."

He followed as she led him round the side of the house to a section which had been built on at a later date.

"This used to be what is called a granny flat," she explained as she put a key in the lock. "The man who owns the house built it for his mother. When she died they decided to let it."

It was a strange feeling to be ushered into the place where your own wife lived. Martin was silent, looking about him as she switched on the lights. 'Flat' was a flattering term for the quarters Sue now occupied. It really consisted of a tiny hall, off which opened the kitchen, bathroom and a not very large bed-sitter.

He sensed that she was self-conscious and embarrassed as he went in. She hurried past him to put away a few odd articles of clothing which she had left lying around. But even though the furniture was the landlord's Sue had put her own stamp on it, giving the room a few feminine touches which made it quite charming. He could not help comparing its neat orderliness with the chaos of his own flat. The flowers on the centre table were unmistakably fresh.

She was rummaging in a cupboard and now produced a bottle and two glasses.

"I've got some brandy. Will that do?"
"That's fine. But you're the one who needs it."

He remained standing while she poured out the drinks. The neck of the bottle rattled on the glasses. Either she too was embarrassed or the shock had not worn off. She handed him the glass, but did not ask him to sit down.

He watched her drink half her glass of brandy, then said: "I'm sorry, Sue, but I want you to go over your story again —"

"But, Martin, I've told you. It's nearly ten o'clock and I'm desperately tired."

"I can't help that. There's been a murder, the third in a couple of weeks. You understand what that means for me. You know how I work. I like to go through every detail. Not once, but half a dozen times."

"But I've told you everything that happened," she said with exasperation.

"Tell me again, Sue."

She heaved a sigh. "From the beginning?"

"Please," he insisted quietly. "Right from the beginning."

"Very well, then." Sue seemed to have resigned herself to giving a more coherent account of what had happened. As she talked she moved restlessly about the room as if reluctant to seat herself under the scrutiny of Martin's searching eyes. "After I telephoned you I changed my mind about not meeting you at the cottage. I don't know why, Martin. I think perhaps I had a guilty conscience because I'd been rude to you on the 'phone."

"You weren't rude, Sue."

"Anyway, I caught the bus out to Stansfield and then walked up to the cottage. I was about half-way up the path when I suddenly realised that the front door was open . . ."

"Wide open?"

"No, but just wide enough to see into the hall. Naturally I jumped to the conclusion that you were in the cottage." She took another sip from her glass and put it on one of the small tables.

"Go on, Sue."

"As I walked through the front door I had a curious feeling that it wasn't you in the cottage after all. I was just about to call 'Where are you, Martin?' when a man jumped from behind the door and grabbed me by the throat. I struggled and was actually on the verge of passing out when the man suddenly pushed me on one side and rushed into the living-room."

Martin nodded. "He'd realised by then that you weren't Mrs. Bodley."

"I suppose so. Anyway, I rushed out of the cottage and ran all the way to the call-box. About twenty minutes later Sergeant Kennedy picked me up."

"Thank you, Sue." The brief account had been more comprehensible than the disconnected snippets of information she'd given him in the car. "Now tell me again exactly what happened when the man suddenly . . ."

"Martin, it's no use!" She was facing him angrily across the settee. "I've told you. I didn't see him. I didn't even catch a glimpse of him."

"But he got hold of you," he insisted. "You must have felt his hands, his coat, his face. There must be something about him you remember."

"Martin, I'm sorry. I know this is important and I'd like to help. But it's no use my just making things up . . ."

"That's the last thing I want you to do." He tried hard to control his impatience. "But there must be something you remember about him. It doesn't matter how trivial — how unimportant. For instance, how tall was he?"

"I don't know." She shook her head and he noted the obstinate set of her face. She was probably trying to block a horrifying memory out of her mind.

"As tall as me?"

"I just don't know."

"What sort of clothes was he wearing?" he asked, trying another tack.

"Martin, I've told you, I can't remember a single thing — about the man —"

She was staring unseeingly at the vase of fresh flowers, whose perfume was faintly discernible. The two vertical lines between her eyebrows had deepened, a sure sign that she was making an effort to remember something.

"What is it?"

"It's nothing. It was just that . . ."

He was sure that she was on the point of recalling some important detail. He moved round the settee and took hold of her arms, his hands under her elbows.

"Sue."

"I think . . ." She was searching his face with extraordinary intensity.

"Go on."

"I think perhaps he — uses the same after-shave lotion —"

"After-shave? Do you mean — the same as me?"

"Yes. But I'm not sure, I'm not sure at all. It's a long time since . . ."

Her face was very close to his, closer than at any time since they had separated. The hostility and remoteness had gone. Her eyes were hurt and frightened, her mouth had fallen into its natural shape, rather like when she was asleep. Suddenly his arms had gone round her and his lips were pressed against hers. She relaxed against him, her mouth soft and yielding. Then she seemed to realise what was happening, raised her arms and pushed him away. He released her and stood back.

"Well?" His voice was tense. "Is it the same?"

"You shouldn't have done that!" she said angrily.

"Answer me!" He seized her arms again and gave her a shake. "Is it the same after-shave?"

Sue's anger had been brief She turned her head away, avoiding the challenge of his eyes. She seemed to give the question careful consideration before she looked up directly into his face.

"Yes," she said slowly. "Yes, I think it is."

He released her, not wanting to push things any further at this stage. "Thank you, Sue," he said and picked up his hat from the chair.

She stood watching him thoughtfully as he went to the door and, with a final parting nod, disappeared into the hall. A moment later the bang of the front door told her that she was alone again.

At eleven o'clock in the morning the High Street in Guildfleet was bustling with activity. The FULL sign had gone up outside the most central car park and the traffic wardens were having a field day with the cars of impatient owners who had parked on the yellow line. A huge articulated lorry was standing outside the supermarket. Four men in white coats with trolleys were unloading the cardboard cartons and trundling them in through the goods entrance. Opposite the bank a Securicor van was pulled up, its open rear door guarded by a tough-looking man wearing a protective helmet. The placards propped against the newsvendor's stand proclaimed 'New Guildfleet Murder', 'Local Woman Found Strangled'.

A couple of pavement photographers were working their way up the street, snapping likely buyers and thrusting their little cards at them. Most people ignored the offer but a few unwisely stopped and let themselves be talked into ordering copies of the photographs. The photographers did not get much change from the couple who emerged from the supermarket. They were laden with parcels and enjoying some private joke. The woman was the youngish, buxom type and the man at her side was tall and bespectacled. He wore a worn tweed jacket and baggy trousers which contrasted sharply with the flashy appearance of his companion. He shook his head emphatically as the photographer clicked his camera and thrust a card at him. The laugh froze on his face as he saw the traffic warden peering at the number-plate of a shiny Ford Capri parked opposite. Defying the traffic, he ran across the road to try and talk her out of writing the ticket.

Martin Denson had walked from the nearest car park with available space. As he emerged from the alley which connected it to the High Street one of the photographers raised his camera and took his picture. Martin waved the proffered card aside with a frown of annoyance. He turned left and was just passing the local branch of W.H. Smith & Sons when a man came out. He had unfolded the newspaper he had just bought and was so intent on the headlines that he almost cannoned into the Inspector.

"I beg your —" He had begun the apology before he saw who it was. When he realised it was Martin he switched on an affable smile. "Oh hello, Inspector."

"Good morning, Mr. Norton. This is a surprise! I was trying to get you on the 'phone about twenty minutes ago."

"I do take time off — occasionally, Inspector."

"I imagine you do, sir. And I can't say I blame you. I just can't think of anything worse than teaching people how to drive!"

"Your job isn't exactly a sinecure, by the look of things." Roy tapped the paper with the back of his hand.

"You mean — Mrs. Bodley?"

"Yes. What happened, Inspector?"

"It's in the paper, sir."

As Martin moved away along the footpath, Roy fell into step beside him.

"Yes, I know, but — it says here that she was strangled."

"That's right."

"In your cottage?"

"That's correct."

"Well, it's none of my business, of course, but — do you think this had got anything to do with — what happened to Judy Clayton?"

"Yes. Yes, I do, sir."

Martin's neutral tone had given the inquisitive Roy little encouragement to persist with his questions. He now deliberately changed the subject.

"Mr. Norton, I'll tell you why I tried to get in touch with you. I'm a shade puzzled about what happened the other night, the night you had dinner with Mrs. Walker."

"What is it you're puzzled about?" Roy asked in his most plausible and helpful voice.

"I understand you suddenly decided to make a 'phone call." Martin had stopped at a zebra crossing and was waiting for the traffic to give him precedence. "From your office."

"That's right."

"Why from your office, sir? Why not 'phone from the hotel?"

An approaching car stopped and the two men crossed the street. Roy was smiling wryly as they gained the footpath on the other side. His manner suggested that he was really very glad to have the chance to explain himself.

"I've had a feeling you'd get round to that telephone call sooner or later, Inspector. The fact of the matter is, a client of mine — Lady Talbot — was taking her test the next morning and I suddenly remembered a piece of advice I wanted to give her. I couldn't remember her number — she's ex-directory — so I had no alternative. I had to go back to the office."

"I see," Martin said non-commitally. "I take it Lady Talbot was an important client?"

"Very. And she still is." Roy laughed. "She failed — for the fourth time."

Martin had stopped outside the tobacconist's he habitually patronised. He favoured Roy with his most impassive look.

"It's perhaps a pity you telephoned her, sir."

Roy's brow furrowed as he tried to decide whether this was a friendly joke or a warning with more sinister undertones. Martin turned his back and went into the shop.

Arthur Eastwood heard the front door of Gameswood House close behind him as he went down the steps. He relieved his pent-up frustration and anger a little by muttering an oath which consigned all women to a very unpleasant place. Gripping the briefcase tightly, he stumped towards his car, which was parked in the drive about twenty yards away. He had opened the door and thrown the briefcase onto the passenger's seat when he heard another car turn in at the gates. Feeling sure that it must be Roy Norton he did not get into the car but stood there waiting. He felt in the mood to have it out with the fellow right here and now.

But it was Inspector Denson's car which rolled into view and stopped opposite the steps.

"Good morning, Inspector," he called out, as Martin got out of the car.

"Good morning, sir." Martin tilted his head towards the house. "Is Mrs. Walker in?"

"Yes, but you won't find her in a very receptive mood, I'm afraid."

"I very rarely find anyone in a receptive mood these days, sir. Is she alone?"

"That's a good question." Arthur spoke bitterly. "There's no one with her, if that's what you mean. But, I regret to say, Mr. Norton's there in spirit, if not in person."

"It sounds as if you've got problems," said Martin, smiling at Arthur's acid tone.

"You can say that again! And bloody silly problems at that!" He shook his head and glanced towards Heaven for commiseration. "She's got a perfectly good lawyer and a perfectly good accountant and yet, for some obscure reason, she chooses to ignore both of them."

"They're obviously not as charming as Mr. Norton."

"Or as persuasive." Arthur pulled the door of his car open and prepared to manoeuvre his ample form behind the steering wheel. "Well, I suppose some women are just naturally stupid!"

"That's right, sir. And some are under-rated."

Arthur twisted round but Martin was already walking towards the front door. He stared at the Inspector's back and opened his mouth to make some comment. Then abruptly he changed his mind, slammed the door and rammed the ignition key into the slot.

Evelyn Walker was entirely composed when she opened the door and found Inspector Denson standing outside. He guessed that she had already seen him from the window of the dining-room, which looked out over the front. Her hair had been recently set and her make-up was fresh. Apart from the plain grey cosrume she was wearing, she did not exactly fit the picture of a grief-stricken widow.

"Good morning, Mrs. Walker. I wonder if you could spare me a few minutes ?"

"Yes, of course, Inspector," she replied at once and stepped back, holding the door open. "Mr. Eastwood's just left me. Perhaps you met him in the drive."

"Yes. We exchanged a few words."

He followed her as she led him into the drawing-room. He noticed that the paper lay open on the coffee table in front of the settee, displaying the same headlines as had so fascinated Roy Norton.

"Can I get you a drink? Sherry perhaps, or a gin and tonic?"

"No, thank you, Mrs. Walker. But I will sit down, if I may. I've been on my feet all morning."

"Yes. Of course."

He put his coat and hat on an upright chair near the door and seated himself on the settee. Evelyn took a high-backed wing-chair at right angles to him and crossed her shapely legs. She waited politely for him to come to the point.

"The night your husband — died," Martin said, choosing his words carefully, "you were very distressed, and naturally so. Of course, I accepted what you told me as the whole truth."

Her eyes had moved to focus on his face, but she did not turn her head.

"Under the circumstances I did not want to question you closely. I was more worried about your own state of health. But, now that you have had plenty of time to think about it, I wonder if you would care to make any alterations or additions to the statement you made then."

"I'm sorry, Inspector," she said, with innocent bewilderment, "but I just don't understand what you're getting at."

"Then let me put it to you in a different way, Mrs. Walker. When I told you about the note that your husband was supposed to have left . . ."

"*Supposed* to have left?"

Martin ignored the interruption. " . . . you seemed surprised, the inference being that you knew nothing about the note."

"That's right." She was still perfectly composed, her eyes not flinching away. "I didn't know anything about it."

"Well, that's what I'm getting at. You knew nothing about the note — and yet, curiously enough, your fingerprints were on it."

The only sign of tension he noted was a faint heightening of the colour in her cheeks, though the fingers of her right hand began to tap angrily on the arms of the chair. "You must be mistaken, Inspector. I just don't see how they could possibly be on it. Unless of course . . ." She sucked her cheeks in slightly and thoughtfully stared at the picture on the wall behind his head.

"Go on."

"I was in such a state, so frightened . . . I suppose I could have picked the note up without realising what I was doing."

Once again she had assumed the pose of the fragile woman, as prone to error as any other mortal.

"On reflection, I think that's probably what happened, Mrs. Walker," Martin assured her, nodding several times.

She gave him her most attractive smile. "Well, I'm sorry if I made things difficult for you, Inspector."

"It can't be helped. Not to worry. To tell you the truth, the note didn't convince me anyway."

"Because it was typed?"

"Not only because it was typed, but because . . ." Martin leaned forward, clasping his hands and resting them on his knees. "Mrs. Walker, may I talk to you frankly, and in confidence, about your husband?"

"Yes, of course."

"In my opinion, Mr. Walker didn't commit suicide; he was murdered." He tapped the newspaper on the low table in front of him. "Murdered by the same man that killed Mrs. Bociley."

She stared at him, her eyes widening in astonishment. "Are you sure of this?"

"Yes, I'm — pretty sure."

"Well — who is this man?" she demanded. "Why haven't you arrested him?"

"We haven't sufficient proof, Mrs. Walker — not yet, at any rate." He had been looking at the paper. Now he switched to her face and abruptly changed the subject. "The night your husband was murdered you had dinner with Roy Norton at The Bear Hotel."

"That's right. I did."

"When I questioned you about that, when I asked you if Mr. Norton . . ."

"I know — I said Roy had been with me the whole evening." She shrugged and again her fingers began drumming on the arm of the chair. "I'm sorry about that. It was only afterwards that I remembered that he'd left me for about half an hour."

"To go back to his office and make a 'phone call?"

"Yes."

"After he'd made the call, did you notice any difference in him?"

"Difference? In What way?"

"Was he agitated, or worried, or out of breath, perhaps?"

"No, not that I can recall. I'm afraid I was the one that was agitated."

"Because he'd been away from the table so long?"

"Yes. When he left he just said he was going to make a 'phone call. Naturally I assumed he was going to make it from the hotel."

"Did you believe his story — about going back to his office?"
"Why, yes! Of course I did."

"It never occurred to you that he might possibly have gone somewhere else?"

"No, it didn't. Where else could he have . . ." She broke off, startled by a new thought. "You're surely not suggesting that he came here, to see David?"

"I'm not suggesting anything, Mrs. Walker."

Martin let the subject drop there. He stood up and walked towards the window. She watched him as he stood there looking out at the garden. She sensed that he was trying to make up his mind about something. When he turned round his manner had changed completely. It was almost apologetic.

"Mrs. Walker, I shouldn't say this, it's very unprofessional, but . . . I need your help."

"Well — if I can help you, I will of course, Inspector." Evelyn's confidence had returned.

"I'd be grateful if you'd give me some information about someone — someone you know."

"Mr. Norton?"

"No, not Mr. Norton. Someone else . . ."

Ten minutes later Evelyn was showing the Inspector out of the house. Her self-control did not crack till she had closed the door on him. Then she leaned with her back against it for a moment before hurrying into the dining-room to make sure that he was really getting into his car. As the engine started, she left the window and ran across the hall back to the drawing-room. Without sitting down she snatched up the telephone and dialled a number.

The dialling tone sounded six times before a man's voice answered.

"It's me," she said at once. "Now, listen! You're in trouble. Denson's been here. He's just left. He's on to something —"

"I told you not to ring me here till this blows over. He didn't mention my name, did he?"

"Yes, he did. He asked me a lot of questions about you —"

"Right," he cut in. "Don't say any more. There's another extension on this 'phone. He's probably asking everyone questions. There's no need to get worried —"

"But of course I'm worried!"

"Do you want to meet me and talk about this?"

"WELL, THAT'S UP TO YOU."

"I'll come round to your place this afternoon. Suit you?"

"Wait a minute." She broke off to look at her watch. "I've got an appointment at half-past two but I'll be back here by four —"

"Four fifteen then?"

"Yes. All right. I'll be here."

She put the receiver down, opened the silver box on the table and groped for a cigarette. She lit it with the lighter on the mantelpiece, then went to the drinks cupboard and poured herself a neat whisky. She stood there, alternately sipping the liquid and drawing deeply on the cigarette.

Harry Kennedy was sitting on the edge of the desk in Martin's office, studying a report from the forensic department. He was finding it hard to concentrate and wished he hadn't let himself be talked into having that extra pint with his lunch.

He straightened up and blinked his eyes sharply a few times as he heard the unmistakable quick step of the Inspector in the corridor outside. Martin was already taking off his coat as he came in through the door.

"Hello, Harry. Any messages?" he asked, making for the cupboard where the clothes-peg was.

"Yes, a man called Mailer 'phoned." Kennedy replaced the report on the pile of papers on the desk.

"When was this?"

"Oh, about an hour ago. He's ringing back."

"Good." Martin crossed to his desk and looked at the pile of papers without enthusiasm. "Have Bellinger and Turner arrived?"

"Yes, they're in my office."

"I want to see them — straight away."

"Right." Kennedy got to the door before he was struck by an alarming thought. "Mailer . . . That wouldn't be Chief Superintendent Mailer, by any chance?"

"Yes, that's right," Martin answered, his concentration directed on the report in front of him.

"Oh, hell!"

"What the matter?" Martin looked up, smiling at Kennedy's rueful expression.

"He caught me at a bad moment. I was terribly off-hand with him."

"Don't worry, he's probably labouring under the delusion you're highly efficient."

"Is he a friend of yours?"

"Yes, I've known him for many years. He started me in this game. If it hadn't been for dear old Rupert I'd probably be in the Navy by now." Martin pushed his chair back and came out from behind the desk. To Kennedy's relief he was relaxed and friendly. "Are you doing anything this evening, Harry?"

"Nothing special." The Sergeant was slightly baffled by the question. "Why?"

"I want to talk to you. Drop in for a drink about half-past seven."

"Yes — all right," Kennedy agreed, wondering whether he dared ask what this sudden desire to socialise was caused by.

At that moment the telephone rang. Martin picked it up and Kennedy went out, leaving the door half open. Still worried about his casual treatment of a Chief Superintendent, he stopped just outside where he could clearly hear what Martin said.

"Hello? Yes, speaking . . . Oh, hello, Rupert! I was just going to 'phone you. Any news? Yes, I'm listening . . . That's interesting . . . No, I must admit I'm not — not completely. I see . . . Rupert, tell me — how long do you think she's known Stenhouse? . . .Six months? That's not very long . . . Who introduced her to him, do you know? . . . I see . . . What's that? . . . Yes, I should think it's a distinct possibility, and not only with Stenhouse . . . I certainly Thank you, Rupert, you've been a great help — as usual . . . Give my love to Joan . . ."

His fears allayed, Kennedy moved away as he heard the receiver go down. He knew where to find Bellinger and Turner. They'd be playing darts in the station's restroom.

Martin was already showing impatience as the three detectives entered his office.

"Well — how did it go?" he asked Bellinger without preamble.

"Not bad. Not at all bad." Bellinger put a manilla folder on the desk. "What's Cecil Beaton got that we haven't got?"

"I'll tell you when I've seen the photographs."

Martin extracted half a dozen postcard-size photos from the folder and laid them out on his desk. Kennedy came round behind him to look at them over his shoulder. They had mostly been taken in Guildfleet that morning, the subjects never suspecting that the brash street photographers were a couple of CID experts. The first showed Andy Mason and Olive, the former's face just registering his initial reaction to seeing the traffic warden about to book him. There was Roy Norton hurrying into W.H. Smith's, Arthur Eastwood walking along the footpath, his head bowed in thought. Evelyn Walker was just posting a letter at the post office; she was very photogenic and looked extremely attractive despite her serious expression. The only print which did not have the High Street as its background featured Colonel Reams. He was riding his horse somewhere on Kingswood Downs and had just seen the photographer. To judge by his angry face he was in the mood to give the intruder a horse-whipping.

"They're good," Martin commented approvingly. He picked them up in his hand, fanning them out like a poker player, shuffling the order as if he was calculating a bet. "Very good. Thank you, Bellinger — Turner."

"Reams spotted us, I'm afraid."

"Yes. That's evident. Well, it can't be helped." He handed the snapshots back to Bellinger, who had realised that the Inspector had deliberately put them in a certain order. "You know what to do now?"

"Yes. We've been to Kingswood village, sir. We made a list of every chemist within a radius of twenty miles." Bellinger withdrew a folded paper from his pocket. "There's a devil of a lot of them, I'm afraid."

"That doesn't matter. Check every one." Martin turned to Kennedy. "Have you given them the lipstick?"

"Yes, I've got it, sir." Turner took a lipstick out of his pocket and held it up for Martin to see.

"Do we show them all the photographs, Inspector?" asked Bellinger, who was holding the bunch just as the Inspector had given them to him.

"Show them the one on top first. It's my bet they'll recognise him. If they don't, then show them the others."

Kennedy moved round behind Bellinger to see which photograph was uppermost. He stared at Martin incredulously. The Inspector gave a small nod of confirmation.

Harry Kennedy was still wondering why the Inspector was suddenly so keen to have his company. It was not as if they did not see enough of each other at the station or on the numerous sorties they made together in the CID car. Perhaps Martin was beginning to feel the pinch of loneliness now that he had been living alone for so long. Kennedy never had understood why he and Sue had broken it off. She must surely have known what she was taking on when she married a policeman. It was such a waste of two nice people. Harry's devotion to his own Dorothy did not prevent him awarding Sue high points for feminine appeal and, though he would never have admitted it, he had an almost fanatical admiration for Martin.

When he rang Martin's door bell at precisely half-past seven the Inspector greeted him with friendliness but also a certain shyness which he had never shown any sign of before. They chatted about the latest developments in the case while Martin poured a glass of brown ale for his guest. Kennedy was by preference a draught bitter man, but beer is always beer. Martin, to the Sergeant's disgust, poured himself a plain tonic water. The Inspector had been known to drink, but usually after a case had been cracked.

With the Sergeant comfortably installed in an armchair, Martin sat on the arm of the sofa. Kennedy, knowing that he was about to broach the reason for this invitation, waited for him to speak.

Martin cleared his throat in slight embarrassment. "Well, I didn't get you here to talk shop, Harry. I want you to do something for me."

"Yes, of course. What is it?"

Martin paused, still hesitant, then took an envelope from his side pocket. "I've written a letter to Sue. I want you to keep it, for the time being at any rate." He handed Kennedy the letter, then stood up and went towards the kitchen. "If anything should happen to me in the next week or so, give it to her."

"What do you mean, if anything should happen to you?" Kennedy had to address his question to Martin's back.

"Well, you know our business, Harry. There's always an outside chance that something unpleasant might happen."

Kennedy looked at the sealed envelope. On it was written the one word 'Sue'. He put his drink down, stood up and followed Martin into the kitchen. "What are you up to?"

Martin had opened the door of the fridge and was extracting one of the ice trays.

"All I'm asking you to do is to give Sue that letter, if I'm unlucky enough to . . ."

"Look, Martin, don't give me that. What the hell are you up to?"

"I saw Mrs. Walker this morning and — I took a risk. A calculated risk." He had carried the ice tray to the sink and was pouring warm water over it. "Personally, I think it'll come off, but if it doesn't, well — it's just possible that something might happen to me, in which case I'd like Sue to have that letter."

"All right," Kennedy agreed grudgingly. "I'll see she gets it." He studied the letter with a worried frown then burst out: "Martin, why the devil do you always have to break every rule in the book?"

Martin eased a cube of ice out of the tray and dropped it in his drink. When he turned to face Kennedy his blue eyes were innocent.

"What book, Harry?"

Kennedy finally ran Sue to earth in one of Guildfleet's newest restaurants. It was called The Mandarin and had quickly established a reputation for serving good but inexpensive Chinese food. Sue was ensconced at a corner table surrounded by the small bowls of delicacies which inevitably accompany Chinese dishes. A diminutive and ageless Chinese was just beginning to take the dishes away and Sue was wiping her mouth with the paper napkin.

She looked up in surprise when she saw Kennedy threading his way through the dimly lit room towards her, his overcoat draped on his arm. His hair was glistening with raindrops from a passing shower.

"Why, hello, Harry!" she greeted him, with a smile of genuine pleasure, and closed the paperback novel she had been reading.

"My word, you're a difficult woman to find, Sue! I was beginning to think you'd emigrated!" He indicated the vacant chair opposite her. "May I sit down?"

"Yes, of course. I was just going to order coffee. Will you join me?"

"Thanks." Kennedy let the little waiter take his coat and sat down. "I've been looking all over the place for you. If I hadn't bumped into your boss I'd never have found you."

"My boss?"

"Mr. Eastwood. I went to the factory and he said you'd been working late and were probably having a meal somewhere."

"What is it, Harry?" Sue said with concern, realising that something was wrong. "What has happened?"

"Nothing, really. I just wanted to have a chat, that's all."

She raised a hand to attract the waiter's attention. "Do you like your coffee black or white?"

"Black, please." As she gave the order Harry tilted his head to try and see the title of the novel on the table in front of her. "What's the book?"

"How to read people's thoughts in ten easy lessons'! Now come on, Harry! What is it? What's this all about?"

Kennedy ran his fingers through his hair before leaning forward confidentially with his elbows on the table. "I'm worried, Sue," he said quietly.

"About what?"

"About Martin."

"That makes two of us," she said drily.

"Sue, please listen to what I've got to say." He spoke with quiet insistence. "I think Martin knows who murdered Judy Clayton, but since he hasn't got sufficient evidence to make an arrest he's taking a risk. A risk he wouldn't dream of taking under normal circumstances."

"I'm sorry, Harry, I'm not with you. I don't understand what you're getting at."

Sue had extracted her cigarette case from her bag and was busily lighting up.

"What I'm trying to say is this: Martin's playing a lone game. He's doing things he wouldn't dream of doing if you and he were still together, Sue."

"Martin's always played a lone game." Sue blew the first cloud of smoke past his shoulder. "He's always done precisely what he wanted to do. You know that as well as I do, Harry. That's one of the reasons we split up."

"Yes, I know. He's a selfish cuss and he always will be . . ." "I didn't say that," she interrupted sharply.

" . . .but he's been a very good friend to me, Sue, and I'd hate to think that anything could happen to him just because I hadn't the guts to . . ." He hitched his chair closer to the table. "Look, do me a favour! Talk to him! Try and get the stubborn so-and-so to realise he's not in business on his own."

"Anything I say wouldn't have the slightest effect on him."

"I think it would. If I didn't think so, I wouldn't be here."

Kennedy leaned back as the waiter materialised and put two tiny cups in front of them. Sue put a sugar-lump into her cup and began to stir it thoughtfully.

"You said just now . . . 'I'd hate to think anything could happen to him . . .'"

"Yes." Kennedy waited, watching the changing expression of her face.

"What could happen to him?"

"What happened to Judy Clayton — to Mrs. Bodley. What very nearly happened to you. If this man thinks Martin's got information about him — information he's fool enough to keep to himself — he won't hesitate to strike."

"But surely Martin must realise that?"

"It's a risk he's prepared to take."

Sue lifted her cup, her eyes guarded as she looked at him over the top of it. "Well, I just don't see what I can do, Harry."

"I've told you what you can do. You can talk to him." His forehead was furrowed as he debated with himself whether he should make this next move or not. Then abruptly he put his hand in his pocket. "He gave me this letter. It is for you. He told me to give it to you if anything happened to him. I think for his sake, as well as yours, you should read it now." He handed the letter across the table, and watched unhappily as she ripped it open and withdrew the closely-written sheets of paper. "He'll tear me apart for this . . ."

Martin would never have fallen for such an old trick if he had not been concentrating on his search for that receipt. After Kennedy's departure he had cooked himself a scratch supper, then settled down to listen to one of his collection of records before turning in. It was a good many days since he had been able to get to bed before the early hours and he knew he had a lot of sleep to catch up on. He had already undressed and put on his pyjamas when he noticed the paper he had propped on his dressing-table. It was a 'final notice' for the telephone bill on the cottage. He was certain he had paid it at the post office, but he had been unable to lay his hands on the receipt. Determined to settle the matter there and then he put on his dressing-gown and resigned himself to making a proper search.

The best bet was the bottom drawer of his writing desk. A mass of papers had been shoved in there as soon as he had moved the bureau from the cottage to his flat. He squatted down and began to remove the bundles of documents. The drawer was nearly empty and the documents were laid out on the carpet round him in a semi-circle when the door bell rang sharply.

Martin glanced at his watch. It showed twenty minutes past ten. Rather late for a social call but not too late for Kennedy to come round if he had any fresh news.

He straightened up, pulled the dressing-gown cord tighter round his middle and went through the hall. As soon as he opened the door he felt the draught go past his legs, a sure sign that the door on the ground floor had been opened. There was no one on the landing outside, merely a brown paper parcel which had been deposited on the mat. As he stared at it the draught ceased and he knew that the door below had been closed. He assumed that who-ever had left the parcel had beat a hasty retreat.

Always suspicious of unidentified parcels, he crouched down to take a closer look at it before he touched it. At once he realised his mistake. As his head crossed the line of the threshold his vision recorded the dim form close against the wall to his right. Martin's reflexes were swift but not swift enough. He saw the arm descend-ing gripping a revolver by the barrel and flung himself sideways in an attempt to avoid the blow. He was only partially successful. Instead of crashing onto his skull with bone-shattering force, it struck him a glancing blow on the temple, enough to stun him but not knock him completely unconscious. He slumped forward like a boxer who has been laid out but hopes to rise before the count of ten.

The wiry, vicious-looking little man who had been standing beside the door stepped forward, raising the butt of the revolver and taking careful aim at the back of Martin's head. Before he could bring it down a whirlwind hit him.

Sue had been starting the last flight of stairs, the carpet muting her steps, when she heard the door of Martin's flat being opened. As the landing came into view she was just in time to see Martin stoop and his attacker aim a vicious blow at his head. Her horror at seeing her former husband knocked out turned to fury as she saw the man move across and prepare to strike again.

With a shriek of "Stop it! Leave him alone!" she cleared the top steps and flung herself at the assailant.

Gordon Pike had done plenty of jobs on men — at a price. He had never before needed to cope with the female of the species in her most dangerous mood. A killer himself, he realised instinctively that it was his turn to be the prey of a creature attacking with the bared tooth and claw of the jungle. She was coming at him with total disregard for the gun in his hand. Feverishly he tried to reverse his grip so that he could direct the barrel at her, but she got to him while he was still fumbling.

The gun clattered to the floor as he put his hands down to protect his groin from the vicious kick she was aiming at him with her booted foot. The next moment nails scored across his face, narrowly missing his eye. Sue's strength and violence were something he had never expected to meet in a woman. He twisted away, stooping to recover the gun. It had fallen near Martin's foot and before he could reach it, the Inspector kicked it across the landing.

Pike decided he had had enough. Dodging Sue's clawing hands he made for the stairs and started down them like a bolting rabbit. Sue picked the gun up and fired blindly after the diminishing target. She got off two rounds before a hand closed on her arm. She turned and saw Martin, swaying on his feet. He just had the strength to take the automatic out of her hand before his knees buckled. She quickly got an arm under his arm to prevent him falling, and taking his weight against her body, helped him back towards his own doorway.

From down below came the sound of the main door to the flats being violently slammed.

She would not let him talk till she had dealt with the wound on the side of his head. The gun butt had split the skin of his right temple, which was oozing blood. He lay full length on the settee while she fetched a bowl of water and gently cleaned the cut before bandaging it up. He was glad enough to submit and allow his spinning head to steady down. But, more important still, he was very aware that this was a different Sue, more like the one he had first fallen in love with. Her touch was very tender, her eyes sincerely concerned, her voice gentle as she told him about Harry Kennedy giving her the letter.

As she finished the bandage and stood up, Martin struggled into a more upright position.

"I could murder him for giving you that letter."

"If you'd got any sense you'd recommend him for promotion. If he hadn't given me the letter I wouldn't have turned up when I did."

"I realise that, Sue. And please don't think I'm not grateful . . ." "You don't sound very grateful."

"It's just that I didn't want . . ."

"You didn't want me to know what you really felt about me until you were dead!"

"It isn't that, it's just that . . . Well, in a way I suppose . . ." He gave up the attempt to find words. Sue could not help smiling. "Oh, hell!"

"Martin, you're an obstinate, big-headed, egotistical . . ."

"I know! I know! You don't have to tell me. Falling for an old trick like that. As soon as I saw the parcel on the mat I should have . . ." Martin shook his head and immediately winced as a shock of pain lanced through his head. He put a hand up gingerly and touched the bandage round his temple. "Oh, my God . . ."

"Stop talking, Martin. You'll only give yourself a headache."

"What do you think I've got!" His voice was furious but he took care not to move his head. Then, after a pause: "I'd like to get my hands on that character. Sue, do you think you'd recognise him again? If we showed you some photographs, could you pick him out?"

"I'm not sure, I could try."

"I'll get Harry to lay it on tomorrow morning." He swung his legs to the floor as a first move in getting onto his feet. "Do you know, I think I'll have a drink. It'll make me feel better."

"Martin, don't be ridiculous!" She moved to him quickly, and put a hand on his shoulder to prevent him standing up. "The best thing you can do is take that dressing-gown off and get into bed."

"I don't want to go to bed. Sue, stop fussing! I'll be all right." He did not see the hurt on her face because she had turned away to pick up her coat.

"Well, if you're all right, I'll be making a move. Is there anything else you want before I go?"

"What d'you mean — before you go?" Martin demanded in almost comic alarm. "You can't leave! I might pass out. I might even go into a coma!"

"My bet is, the moment I walk out of that door you'll head straight for the kitchen and get yourself a beer."

He reached out and took hold of her arm. "Sue, don't go — not yet. Please . . ."

She did not pull her arm away, but came closer and sat on the arm of the settee. "Martin, why did that man try to kill you?"

"He was paid to kill me."

"By whom?"

He considered the question for a moment, then made up his mind to confide in her.

"For some time now I've had a pretty shrewd idea who murdered Judy Clayton. This morning, without actually spelling it out, I told Evelyn Walker enough to make her realise that
I knew. I also told her I was keeping the information to myself, for the time being at any rate."

"Why did you do that?"

"Can't you guess?"

"You mean — she knows the murderer and she tipped him off?" Martin nodded. "In other words, you deliberately fed her the information?"

"Yes."

"But what made you go to Mrs. Walker? How did you know she was involved in this affair?"

"A little while ago, when we were talking about her, you said: 'I don't know why, but . . . I always have the feeling that she's not quite what she seems to be' . . ."

"Did I say that?" Sue seemed surprised and at the same time pleased that he had remembered a casual remark of hers well enough to quote it verbatim.

"Yes. And from that moment I decided to investigate her. I even telephoned Rupert Mailer and asked him to find out what he could. You were right, Sue. Roy Norton isn't the only character she's been jumping into bed with. She's been having an affair with a man called Jack Stenhouse."

"Jack Stenhouse? But he's a friend of Mr. Eastwood's! I've met him. He was in the office only a few days ago."

"Yes. I know." Martin looked up into her face and indicated the vacant seat beside him. "Why don't you sit down and make yourself comfortable? And do you remember how you used to cure my headaches when I had those migraines?"

"How did I cure them?" Sue asked with a faint smile twitching the corners of her mouth.

"You used to massage the back of my head with your fingers. What about seeing if it still works?"

It was mid-morning when Detective-Constable Bellinger reached the Guildfleet police station. He went straight up to Inspector Denson's office in the CID wing of the building. He was about to knock on the door when Harry Kennedy came out.

"Morning, Jim. You got something for us?"

"I certainly have. Is he in?"

"Denson? He's down in records. I'll tell him you're here if you'd like to go in."

"Do that. What I've got here is going to put him in a good mood."

"He's in a fantastic mood already, Jim. I don't know what's done it, but you'd think he had the case all buttoned up. Somebody swiped him over the head last night. Perhaps that's what caused it."

A few minutes later when Martin breezed into his office he surprised Bellinger surreptitiously reading the letter on the desk. Martin did not miss the movement as he quickly replaced it, nor the young constable's embarrassment at being caught in the act. Instead of frowning, he gave him a friendly smile. Bellinger noted the large patch of sticking plaster on the side of his head.

"Any luck, Bellinger?"

"Yes," Bellinger said, obviously pleased to be the bearer of significant information. "I've just left a young chap called Arthur Grainger. He's got a chemist's shop in a village about a mile from where Walker's car conked out."

"Well?"

"I showed him our friend's photograph. He thinks he served him."

"He thinks?"

"Yes."

"But he's not sure?"

"I think he's sure, but he doesn't want to get involved."

"To hell with that!" Martin said, with a sudden return of his old impatience. Bellinger shifted uncomfortably on his feet.

"He says if it's the same man, he bought a packet of razor blades, some after-shave and a lipstick."

"This Arthur Grainger remembers the lipstick?"

"Yes. This man made a crack about it. Something to do with his girlfriend."

"Good. What about the after-shave?" Martin's keen eyes were fixed on the young man's. "What kind was it?"

"I don't know. I didn't ask him."

"You should have done," Martin said, more in sorrow than in anger.

"You didn't say anything about after-shave, sir. You simply mentioned the lipstick and . . ."

"You'd better go back and ask him, Bellinger. Find out if it was called Sundown — it's made by Timbers, the soap people."

"Yes, right, sir." With most of the wind taken out of his sails Bellinger made for the door, his face crestfallen.

Martin moved round the desk to see what paper had so much attracted his interested. He had barely time to read the letter before Kennedy was back.

"Colonel Reams is here, sir. He'd like a word with you."

"Reams? What's it about, Harry?"

"I don't know. He just said he wanted to see you. I'll talk to him if you like."

"No, I'll see him. Show him in." Martin rose to greet his visitor. Reams came in looking a good deal less sure of himself than in his office. His conciliatory manner was very different from the irate horseman who had threatened the photographers. "Come in, sir. Thank you, Harry."

"It's good of you to see me, Inspector," Reams said, as Kennedy went out.

"Sit down, sir."

"Thank you." Reams sat down, and raised his eyebrows at the dressing on the Inspector's head. "Have you had an accident, Inspector?"

"Sort of," Martin said casually and sat himself on the corner of his desk. "What can I do for you?"

"I thought you might like to know that I called in my local garage yesterday afternoon and the chap who owns it, a man called Aldrich, started talking about Tom. He was a friend of Tom's, and Ruth Jensen's, too."

"About what?"

"Tom's car. Tom said he intended to sell it to Ruth and Aldrich told him it was a pretty rotten trick."

"Why should he say that?"

Reams had produced his gold case and was preparing to light a cigarette. "Because apparently, although the car looked all right, it was really a dreadful old banger."

"I see." Martin picked up his desk lighter and snapped the flame on for Reams to light up. "In other words, you think that explains what Ruth was doing in the car?"

"Well, yes." Reams leaned back in his chair and crossed his legs. "And it also explains how the accident happened."

"You mean Tom was taking her for a trial run and showing off the car?"

"Knowing Tom, I'd call it plain showing off."

"It sounds a likely explanation, I must admit." Martin regarded Reams thoughtfully for a few seconds then stood up to indicate that he considered the interview over. "It was kind of you to put me in the picture, sir."

"Yes, well, I thought perhaps I'd better tell you about it." Reams leaned forward in his chair but he did not actually stand up.

"You did the right thing, sir. Is there anything else you'd like to tell me while you're here?" Martin's voice was still pleasant, but there was a hint of impatience in it.

"No, I don't think . . . What do you mean?"

"I just wondered if there was anything else you wanted to talk about, sir?"

"No. No, there's nothing else." The Colonel put his hands on his knees and got to his feet. He was about to shake Martin's outstretched hand when he seemed to have second thoughts. "There's just one thing . . ."

"Go on, sir."

"That telephone call — the one that Ruth made — I think perhaps I know why she made it — why she wanted to talk to you." Reams was looking at Martin, but the latter simply stood there, his face showing polite interest and waited for him to go on. "After the murder I made Ruth swear that she wouldn't tell anyone that Tom had been friendly with Judy Clayton. I have a lot of very important clients and I didn't want them to think that I was running the sort of establishment that . . ."

125

"I get the point, sir."

"When you questioned her that morning I reminded Ruth of the promise she'd made. Unfortunately I must have frightened her into thinking that I was covering up for Tom and that — he'd actually committed the murder."

"I see." Martin's monosyllabic replies had given Reams little help. He drew on his cigarette and straightened his shoulders in the well-cut tweed jacket.

"I'm sorry, I suppose I should have told you all this before, Inspector."

"It might have been a little more helpful, sir."

Reams was wondering what to say next when Kennedy knocked and put his head round the door.

"Excuse me. Sue wants to see you."

"Any luck?"

"Yes, I think so. I think she's spotted him."

Reams had listened to the brief exchange with unconcealed curiosity. Martin put an arm out to shepherd him towards the door.

"Thank you, Colonel. We'll be in touch."

Sue was in Kennedy's office, two doors along the corridor. She had been going systematically through the pile of photographs which Martin had brought up from the records office. As her husband came in she and Tomkins were staring at one of the standard photographic records which the police keep of all arrested criminals — one full-face and the other profile.

Sue glanced round and, as Martin came in, held up the photograph for him to see.

"What do you think, Martin?"

He took it and at once recognised the face which had been stamped on his memory in the split second before the butt of the revolver hit him.

"Yes, that's him. That's him all right. Thank you, Sue." "His name's Pike, sir," Tomkins supplied. "Gordon Pike." Martin asked Kennedy: "Do you know him?"

"I do. He's a vicious little devil. He was accused of attacking and robbing an old lady in Surbiton, about six months ago. But we couldn't make it stick. He was acquitted."

"Pick him up, Harry!" Martin threw the photograph onto the desk. "We'll make this one stick!"

Sue still had not appeared when Martin arrived at the Mandarin Restaurant for a rather late lunch. He only had to wait a moment before being shown to a table which had just been vacated by two businessmen. For once breaking his rule, he ordered a glass of sherry and sat back, thankful to have a few minutes to order his thoughts. She came in ten minutes later, slightly flushed and breathless.

"I'm sorry I'm late." She took off her coat and silk scarf and let the waiter take them away.

"That's all right, I've just arrived." Martin had stood up to welcome her. "Would you like a drink?"

Sue sat down and hesitated while she tried to make up her mind. Martin made the decision for her.

"A dry sherry," he told the waiter firmly.

Sue smiled across the table as he sat down, pushing back a strand of hair which had fallen over her brow.

"It's been one of those mornings. The 'phone never stopped ringing. Incidentally, did you telephone the office? Someone said something about a call from . . ."

"Yes, I did. I had a word with Mr. Eastwood."

"Mr. Eastwood?" she repeated, obviously surprised.

"I wanted to see him." Martin's manner was uncharacteristically vague. "But I've changed my mind, I'm not going to see him after all." He picked up the menu and handed it to her. "What would you like to eat, Sue?"

"Let's have the drink first. We'll order later."

"All right," he agreed.

"How's the face?" She was looking at the dressing on his head with critical eyes. "It doesn't look too bad."

"Still a bit painful," Martin said, touching the place carefully with his fingers. "But improving."

"Did you pick up — er — Pike?"

"No. That's a sore point. We nearly did, then at the last moment he gave us the slip. We'll catch him in the end, don't worry."

He leaned back as the waiter appeared with Sue's glass of sherry. As she thanked the little Chinese, Martin raised his glass. "Skol!"

She reciprocated the gesture.

"What is it that you want to talk about?"

"I'd like you to do something for me. You don't have to, of course, if you don't want to."

"What is it you want me to do?"

He unobtrusively glanced over each shoulder to make sure none of the other customers were close enough to listen, then leaned forward.

"You remember what I told you the other night, about Judy Clayton?"

"You said you knew who killed her."

"That's right."

"Well?"

"Since I spoke to you I've had proof, more positive proof, that I'm right. But I still don't think it's enough for me to go ahead and make an arrest. I've got to frighten him into making just one more mistake."

"But you still haven't told me what you want . . ."

"I've got an idea — a plan. I admit it's crazy, as crazy as hell, but if you're willing to help me, I think it'll work."

Sue glanced down at his hand which had slid across the table to grip her forearm. She hesitated, then gave in to the earnest expression on his face.

"I'll help you. On one condition."

"Oh? And what's that?"

"You've got to take Harry Kennedy, or someone at any rate, into your confidence. You've got to tell them who you suspect and why."

"I've already done that. I spoke to Harry this morning and I've sent a report through to Rupert Mailer."

He could see that she was dubious. He slightly increased the pressure of his fingers. "Honestly, Sue."

"All right. Now what is it you want me to do?"

"I've arranged to have a drink with Arthur Eastwood this evening. I said we'd meet at The Grapevine, it's on his way home."

"Well?"

"I don't want to keep the appointment."

"Very well, I'll deal with it," she said briskly. "That's no problem. I'll simply tell him you're . . ."

"I don't want you to tell him anything, Sue. I want to keep the appointment, instead . . ."

During the busy evening period Andy Mason made it a habit to help Mike and George, the two barmen, deal with the crush of customers who habitually flooded into The Grapevine. It also gave him a chance to listen to the local gossip, have a chat with some of his regulars and quietly imbibe a few gins and French on his own account.

Arthur Eastwood, whose visits were few and far between, had come in at about seven and Andy had served him personally and then stayed to chat. The conversation had soon turned to the machinations of the motor trade. Andy was bitterly complaining about the way the Ford dealer had talked him into buying an automatic.

"You'll like it once you've got used to it, Andy." Arthur Eastwood was perched on one of the stools in front of the bar, his fingers round the glass of whisky.

"I hope you're right, but I've had it a month now and I'm still not happy with it. I wish to heavens I'd stuck to the old gear-lever."

While he talked Andy was keeping an eye on things, making sure that Mike and George weren't keeping any of the customers waiting. Olive was dealing with the cold snacks counter. She had gone into Andy's office on hearing the telephone bell ring.

"You're just an old-fashioned square, Andy."

"I find it so damned awkward not using my left foot all the time."

"You'll get used to it . . ." Arthur broke off and glanced yet again at the door. Andy could see that he was waiting for someone.

"Yes, well, if I don't, I'll flog the damn thing!"

Olive had come out from the door which led to the office and was standing at Andy's elbow.

"Excuse me, Mr. Mason. You're wanted on the telephone."

"Oh. Thank you." He gave Arthur a friendly nod. "See you later."

As Andy went into his office Olive placed her folded arms on the counter and gave Arthur her big smile.

"Good evening, Mr. Eastwood."

"Hello, Olive," Arthur responded, trying not to let his eyes be drawn to Olive's generous bosom.

Andy was expecting a call from Evelyn, but when he picked up the 'phone he heard a high-pitched man's voice.

"That you, Andy? It's me, Gordon. I'm going to need some more cash. The rozzers are on my tail. They nearly nabbed me when I went back to the caravan park. If I hadn't had the scooter I'd never have got away."

Andy put a hand over his free ear. He had left the loudspeaker switched on and the sound of Olive's and Arthur's voices was as loud as Pike's squeaky voice on the 'phone.

"You've had your money, Gordon. We agreed on a price and I've paid it. If you've been stupid enough to leave tracks that's your own look out."

"Don't give me that! Listen, either you fork out another five hundred or I talk."

"Five? You've got to be joking. I might be able to let you have another hundred."

"That's no use to me! I said five and I want it straight away."

"You don't seem to realise that the banks are closed —"

"I told you I want it straight away." Pike's voice faded for a moment, as if he was looking round. "I know you keep plenty of ready cash in that safe of yours."

"Hold on a second." Andy held the receiver away. He had heard something on the loudspeaker connected to the bar which had attracted his attention. When he put the instrument to his mouth he spoke softly but urgently.

"All right, Gordon. I'll fix you up. Meet me in the car park at the back of here in an hour. You know my car. It's a blue Ford Capri. I'll see you."

He hung up immediately, but instead of going through to the bar he stood by the desk, listening.

"Good evening, Mr. Eastwood!"

Arthur swung round on his stool, his face showing his surprise at hearing the familiar voice.

"Why, hello, Sue! I didn't expect to see you here! I'm meeting your husband . . ."

Olive tactfully faded away, moving further along the bar to collect some empty glasses.

"Yes, I know you are, but I'm afraid Martin can't make it, Mr. Eastwood. He's been trying to get hold of you. As a last resort he telephoned me."

"Oh, I see. Well, I'm sorry about this, Sue. I hope it hasn't messed up your evening?"

"No, no, I was coming in this direction anyway."

"Er — would you like a drink?"

"Could I have a gin and tonic?"

"Yes, of coursc."

Sue hitched herself up onto the stool beside Arthur, which had just been vacated. She undid the tie-belt of her coat and let it fall open. In answer to Arthur's signal Olive had returned. She regarded Sue with the quizzical expression of an experienced woman who knows perfectly well why attractive young women come into bars alone.

"A gin and tonic, Olive," Arthur told her, his voice sharpening a little as he saw her expression.

"And ice?"

"Please."

Olive nodded and moved away to mix the drink.

"As a matter of fact," Arthur said, "I was a little surprised when your husband suggested that we meet here. I asked him to come to the office but he didn't seem to want to do that."

"No, I rather gather he wanted to talk to you privately about something."

"I would have thought my office would have been a great deal more private than a public bar."

"So would I!" Sue agreed, laughing. "So would most people. But not Martin!"

"I gather he is a pretty off-beat sort of chap when you get to know him."

"I don't know that I'd call him off-beat, exactly." Sue was looking straight ahead, but she could see Arthur's face in the mirror against the wall. "Incidentally, we've made it up. I'm — going back to him."

"Are you?" Arthur swung round, genuinely delighted. "Well — er — congratulations. I suppose that's the right thing to say, under the circumstances?"

"I hope so," Sue said, and could not help laughing at his suddenly worried frown.

"I'm very glad, Sue. I am, really, my dear. But I hope this doesn't mean you're going to leave us?"

"No, it doesn't. Not for the moment at any rate."

Olive placed a glass with a measure of gin and some ice in it in front of Sue and poured half the bottle of tonic into it. Arthur put down a pound note and received a stack of coins for change.

"You've no idea what Martin wanted to see me about, I suppose?"

"No — except that I imagine it was something to do with the Judy Clayton affair."

"I have a feeling your husband and I think alike about that — in fact I'm sure we do."

"Martin's convinced that the man who murdered Judy Clayton also killed Mr. Walker," Sue said, raising her voice above a sudden burst of laughter from a group of young people at a corner table.

"So am I."

"He's also convinced that it won't be long now before they make an arrest."

"Is he? Well, that's certainly good news," Arthur said enthusiastically. "I sincerely hope he's right."

"So do I, but I'm afraid Martin's always optimistic."

"Yes, but surely, there must be grounds for his optimism?" Sue waited till a couple of new arrivals had ordered their drinks.

"I think it's something to do with a photograph and Judy Clayton's lipstick."

"A photograph?"

"Yes. I don't really understand it." Sue shook her head vaguely. "According to what I've heard, someone took a photograph and the police showed it to a chemist, and apparently the chemist . . ."

"A photograph of what?"

"Of a man, a suspect, presumably."

"I see. Go on."

"Well, that's it. That's all I know."

"But you were going to say something about the chemist?"
"Only that he apparently identified the man."

Arthur swallowed most of the whisky in his glass and savoured the after-taste thoughtfully.

"You've no idea who he is, I suppose?"

"I'm afraid I haven't." Sue's eyes flicked up to the mirror opposite her. "Martin didn't tell me. But then naturally, he wouldn't."

"No. No, of course not."

Arthur realised then that Sue was staring into the mirror with a slightly disconcerted expression. He turned round sharply to find Roy Norton standing at his shoulder.

"Good evening," Roy greeted him with a faintly ironic bow. Arthur ignored the greeting and turned his back on him. Quite unruffled, Roy flashed his carefully rehearsed smile at Sue before addressing Olive.

"Is Mr. Mason about, Olive?"

"Yes. He's in his office."

"Tell him I'd like a word with him." He pointed to a table in one of the alcoves at the back of the lounge. "I'll be over there. And bring me a large scotch, there's a sweetie."

Arthur waited till he had gone, as if his presence polluted the atmosphere too much for reasonable conversation to be possible.

"Are you going back to Guildfleet?" he asked Sue, when Roy was well out of earshot. He had finished his drink and clearly wanted to get away.

"No, I'm calling at the cottage. It's only ten minutes from here."

"You're keeping the cottage now, I imagine?"

"Yes, we are."

Sue was only half way through her drink. She studiously ignored Arthur's restlessness.

"It's very attractive. I've always liked it. I'll drop you there, Sue, if you like. It's on my way home."

"Thank you," she said and turned to look at Andy Mason, who had just come out of his office.

"Mr. Norton wants a word with you," Olive informed him. "He's over there."

"Yes," Andy said, betraying no surprise as he raised a hand to show Roy that he had seen him. He looked towards Sue and she was not quick enough to avoid meeting his eyes for an instant. Andy went to the shelf at the back of the bar and served himself with a double whisky. He drank it quickly, then just stood there. Toying with her glass, Sue knew that he was staring at her in the mirror.

Sue felt very bereft as she watched Arthur Eastwood turn his car and drive back down the lane away from the cottage. Martin had not arrived yet. If he had, his car would have been parked outside the gate or on the short drive leading up to the garage. She pushed open the gate and walked slowly up the path through the front garden. The closed and locked windows of the house stared out at her. It was strange that a place where one had once lived happily could appear so menacing, but she still had not shaken off the nightmare memory of that murderous attack.

She stooped to pull a particularly impudent weed out of the path and as she straightened she thought she saw a movement at one of the windows. Her heart had already started to race before she realised that it was her own reflection. This was one of those very still evenings when sounds even from far away carry quite clearly and those nearer are magnified. A startled blackbird fled down the hedge, shrieking its hysterical alarm call. High in the trees of the nearby copse half a dozen rooks were squabbling in raucous tones. She could see their black shapes fluttering.

Why had Martin chosen this place to meet her and why was he keeping her waiting like this? She knew that she had been instrumental in baiting a trap, though she did not really understand what Martin had in mind. The sense of menace and danger was very strong. She could not forget that look in Andy's eyes. Just for a moment, back there in The Grapevine, she had felt a little like a bird that cannot turn away from the coiled cobra.

As she moved round the side of the cottage past the dining-room window, a rabbit scuttled through the hedge into the field. He had been feeding on the bolting lettuces she had planted months ago. Now the weeds had virtually taken over the whole vegetable garden.

The sound of the car coming fast along the lane reached her plainly. She kept out of sight, some instinct warning her not to reveal her presence till she knew who it was. It braked sharply and stopped. She heard a door slamming, feet running and the click of the front gate. Then a voice called: "Sue!"

Suddenly all her fears seemed ridiculous. She answered: "I'm here," and almost ran round the side of the house. Martin was taken by surprise when she flung herself into his arms.

"Oh, thank goodness it's you. I was beginning to get so frightened."

He held her away from him to study her face with concern. "I'm sorry, I got delayed. How long have you been here?" "About five minutes, I suppose, but it seemed ages. Mr. Eastwood dropped me."

"How did it go?" Martin asked anxiously.

"Very well. At least, I think so. Anyway, I did exactly what you wanted."

"Thank you, Sue. I'm very grateful."

"I'm sure he heard us, Martin. When he came out of the office he could hardly keep his eyes off me."

"Good! You've done splendidly." He drew her close again and gave her a kiss. "Now, let's go back to the flat."

He was holding the gate open for her when she stopped, shaking her head in perplexity.

"What is it, Sue?"

"Andy Mason. I just can't believe it."

"I'll say one thing for you, Sue, you certainly know how to make coffee. That's the first decent breakfast I've had in weeks."

"I can't say my own breakfasts have been anything to write home about. That's the trouble about living alone. It just doesn't seem worth bothering when there's only yourself."

The sitting-room of Martin's flat was already very much tidier. The records and books had been put into some sort of order, the dust had been removed from the upper surfaces of the furniture and Sue had set up a table close to the window where it caught the morning sunshine. Martin was fully dressed except for his jacket, which was hanging over the back of his chair. The large patch of sticking plaster had been replaced by a small, neat one. Sue was wearing his silk dressing-gown.

She reached across the table to pour him a fresh cup of coffee. "Martin, tell me. What do you think will happen?"

"You mean — Andy Mason?"

It was almost the first time the case had been mentioned since the previous evening. They had been too involved in each other, making plans for the future, deciding just what to do to make things work better this time.

"It's difficult to say. I'm hoping, after overhearing your conversation last night, that he'll panic and contact Pike again. That was the point of the operation. In which case, of course, we'll pick them both up."

"But how will that help you?"

"Well, obviously, if Pike talks our troubles are over." he talks."

"He'll talk, make no mistake about that!"

"But supposing Andy Mason doesn't contact Pike and makes a dash for it?"

"Then we'll simply have to arrest him and take a chance with the evidence we've already got."

"I see." Sue rearranged the dressing-gown which had slipped off her knee. "Martin, when did you first realise that he was involved in all this?"

"When the camera was found in Judy Clayton's bedroom," Martin said, buttering another piece of toast. "At first, I must admit, I tried to work out all sorts of complicated explanations as to how Judy got hold of the camera. And then suddenly, one morning, it dawned on me there might be a perfectly simple explanation after all."

"Like Andy Mason being a friend of Judy's and simply giving it to her?"

"Yes. Or alternatively, bribing Mrs. Bodley to plant it in her room."

"Either way, of course, meant that Andy never did lose the camera . . ."

"Correct."

"And that right from the beginning he intended to murder Judy Clayton and then throw suspicion on to his brother-in-law."

"That's right. But don't forget we only heard the story about the camera being stolen from Andy and his sister — no one else."

"But why should he want to incriminate David Walker? I always got the impression he was fond of him."

"That's the impression he gave everyone." Martin put the last bit of toast into his mouth and after helping it down with a drink of coffee, pushed back his chair. "I'll tell you what I think is the most likely way things happened. Andy Mason had been having an affair with Judy Clayton for some time. In those circumstances men are apt to tell women a good deal more than they mean to. Judy may have over-played her hand and tried to cut herself in on one of Andy's little rackets. That was not in itself a sufficient reason for murdering her, but it was good enough for Andy to seize a chance when it was presented to him on a plate."

Martin stood up and put his coat on, patting his pockets to make sure he had his wallet, notebook and pencil.

"But how did he know that Judy Clayton was going to be left alone in David Walker's Bentley?"

"Because he'd planned it. Or rather it was his plan that Judy should be on that crossroads outside The Golden Swan when David went past. He knew that David had caught Evelyn with Roy Norton and hoped to get him on the rebound. Judy was a very attractive girl, you know."

"Yes. So I gather," Sue remarked drily. She removed her hand from the dressing-gown and it slipped away from her knee. She saw Martin's glance and smiled to herself.

"Andy wanted Judy to worm her way into David's confidence for reasons which I've not yet been able to fathom. My guess is that he followed the Bentley to make sure what road David took, then passed him somewhere before Kingswood so that she could be waiting on the corner. No doubt he followed at a discreet distance to make sure David really was taking her up North with him. You can imagine how he felt when the Bentley ran out of petrol and Judy was left alone in it. It was an opportunity such as he had never hoped for. When he'd strangled her and hidden her body in the ditch he hit on the idea of leaving that note —"

"Making it look as if she'd written it with her own lipstick," Sue cut in, to prove that she was keeping up with him. "Whose lipstick was it? If he hadn't planned to murder her then how did he come to have a different lipstick on him?"

"He went and bought it from a chemist in the nearest village, choosing the same kind as Evelyn Walker used. All he had to do was go back and throw it into the ditch. He knew damn well we'd find out that the message had not been written with Judy's lipstick, and from that moment onwards —"

"Never believe a word David Walker said."

"Right. But he realised that in spite of the planted evidence I still was not convinced. That's why he faked the suicide and planted the note. There was a double advantage in that. It also made sure his sister inherited David's share in Cavalier Toys."

"But what about the Cavalier key-ring, and the reference in the diary to her having an appointment with someone?"

"Well, obviously she'd had the key-ring for some time. I expect Andy had given it to her. I gather from what you've told me there's dozens of them floating around." Sue nodded confirmation. "As for the diary mentioning the appointment at 10.30, Andy probably made the entry the murder was committed. It was not a very good imitation of her writing, but I'm afraid I did not tell David Walker that."

"You said just now," Sue stood up and began to pile the breakfast things on the tray, "if Andy makes a dash for it you'll have to take a chance on the evidence you've got."

"Yes, and it's not all that strong, I'm afraid. I think the chemist will probably identify him as the man who bought the lipstick. And there's no doubt in my mind — because of the after-shave lotion — that he attacked you at the cottage and murdered Mrs. Bodley."

"I still don't understand why Mrs. Bodley was murdered."

"It's my bet she was being blackmailed and got scared. She suddenly made up her mind to make a statement to me about it. You remember the story she told me about David Walker — about seeing him in town with Judy Clayton?"

"Yes."

"I don't think that story was true. I think she was acting under instructions."

"Instructions — from whom?"

"From the man who was blackmailing her."

"And you think that was Andy Mason, that it was he who attacked me at the cottage and then killed her."

"I'm sure of it."

Sue had picked up the tray and was heading for the kitchen when a long and urgent peal on the door bell echoed through the flat. She cast an alarmed glance towards the hall, very conscious that Martin's silk dressing-gown did very little to hide her figure.

"Are you expecting anyone?'

"No." Martin automatically glanced at his watch. "It's probably the postman."

139

"Well, give me time to get out of sight just in case it isn't."

She hurried into the kitchen as Martin went through the hall to open the door. Harry Kennedy was standing on the mat, his finger raised to prod the bell-push again. He was dog-tired and had not even had a chance to shave.

"Come in, Harry!" Martin held the door wide. "You're just in time for a cup of coffee. We've only just —"

He stopped when he realised that the Sergeant was distressed and shocked.

"What is it, Harry?"

Kennedy came in and closed the door behind him before he broke his news.

"Mason's dead."

"Dead?" Martin echoed incredulously. cryes.,,

"Well — what happened? What the hell happened?"

"He crashed his car. You know he bought a new Ford Capri about a month ago, one with an automatic gear, and according to all accounts —"

He broke off as he saw Sue coming through the sitting-room. She had recognised his voice and picked up the tension in Martin's question.

"Hello, Sue."

"Hello, Harry. What's happened, Martin?"

"Andy Mason's dead — he's been killed in a car accident." He took Harry by the arm and steered him into the sitting-room. His manner was tense. "Go on, Harry. Tell me how it happened."

"He packed his car up with luggage and left The Grapevine just before midnight. Two of our chaps — Wentworth and Bourne — followed him as far as Henley and then . . .whether he got wind of what was happening or not I don't know . . ."

"They lost him!"

"Yes — he suddenly started to drive like a madman. Went completely berserk! We had a call from Windsor about — oh, I should say a quarter to six. Apparently the car went off the road about six miles this side of Reading. It hit a telegraph pole and must have caught fire instantly. Mason was trapped in the car.

Several lorry drivers stopped and got their fire extinguishers to work, but he was incinerated before anyone could get near the car. Bourne's a pretty tough customer, but even he was shaken. He said he's never seen a body so disfigured."

"Was he alone, Harry?" Martin was already putting on his coat and searching for his hat.

"Yes."

"What about his baggage and personal effects? Was anything salvaged?"

"It's at Reading. They're holding it. The fire and the extinguishers have made a pretty good mess of it."

"Does Mrs. Walker know about her brother?"

"Yes. She'd like to see you. She wants to make a statement."

Sue had found Martin's hat. He took it from her with a perfunctory nod, then followed Kennedy who was already crossing the hall. At the door he checked, then came back, put his arm round Sue's waist and kissed her.

"You see?" he said, as he reluctantly released her. "I really meant it when I told you things would be different from now on."

The Inspector's impatience was only thinly disguised. Bellinger, standing near the door, exchanged a quick glance with the uniformed clerk who was taking notes. Martin was sitting behind his desk facing Evelyn Walker. She was trying rather unsuccessfully to look attractive and at the same time grief-stricken at the death of her brother. Martin's uncompromising attitude had unnerved her. She could not know that it was only partly due to her reluctance to come to the point. He was also impatient to get down to Windsor and see the detectives who had dealt with Andy Mason's car crash. When that had been done he could write 'case closed' on the file and at last have some time to devote to his own and Sue's affairs.

"It's so unlike Andy to crash his car." She made a brave effort to hold back tears. "He had a pilot's licence as well and he really prided himself on his driving."

"But you still haven't told me what your brother said to Judy

Clayton. He must have given a reason for wanting her to get friendly with your husband."

Evelyn carefully recrossed her legs. "He told her he was a shareholder in Cavalier Toys and pretended that he wanted her to get certain information out of David. The trip up north was to be only the beginning of their association. But you know what happened. The car ran out of petrol and Andy . . . changed his plans."

"Was your brother a big shareholder in Cavalier Toys?"

"No, but between us we had quite a substantial holding, especially after David was killed." She paused for a moment.

"Andy was ambitious, he wanted to become a director of the company but neither my husband or his partner would hear of it. When Andy heard a rumour about a possible take-over bid he made a point of getting to know Jack Stenhouse. Later he . . .introduced me to him."

"And Mr. Norton? Was it your idea to use Roy Norton as a stooge — or decoy, if you like — so that Arthur Eastwood would think that he was a potential trouble-maker, and not your brother?"

"No, it was Andy's idea. Actually I was against it."

Martin's eyebrows went up. She would have had to be very insensitive to think that he believed her. "You appear to have been against quite a few things, Mrs. Walker. Now tell me what happened the night your husband was murdered."

"Andy telephoned David at his hotel and told him I wanted to see him, urgently. This wasn't true, of course. When I got home, after having dinner with Roy Norton, I didn't even know David was in the house — I swear I didn't! It was only when I saw his cigarette case that I realised . . ." Her voice had begun to falter quite convincingly as she recalled that evening when she had come into the empty house alone. She fumbled for a handkerchief in her handbag. "He must have been actually filling his case when . . .Andy appeared . . ." Her head bowed. She touched her eyes with the handkerchief, apparently unable to continue.

Martin contemplated the performance for a few moments, wondering whether a sharp question would make her snap out of it. Then he changed his mind, pushed his chair back and stood up.

"Thank you, Mrs. Walker. That's all for the moment. We'll be getting in touch with you again later."

Ignoring her completely he took his coat and hat from the cupboard and, with a meaningful glance at Bellinger, went out of the office.

As he passed Kennedy's office he opened the door and put his head round it.

"I'm off now."

"Yes, all right, sir." Kennedy stood up respectfully, laying down the typewritten sheet he had been studying. "How did you get on with Mrs. Walker?"

Martin grunted and came into the room. "She switched the tears on and I just couldn't take it. Not today anyway. I'll have another go at her tomorrow, after I've talked to Eastwood. What's that you're reading?"

"It's a list of the stuff Andy Mason had with him. They've just sent it through from Reading."

Martin reached across the desk, picked up the list and ran his eye down it. "They've certainly gone to town."

"Yes, I think they wanted to impress us."

"I'll be a bit late tomorrow morning." Martin smiled as he handed the sheet back. "I'm taking Sue out to the cottage before . . ." He stopped, his eyes focussing on distance as they always did when an important thought struck him. He took the list from Kennedy again.

"What is it?" Kennedy asked, wondering what the Inspector had seen which he had missed.

"There's something missing . . ." Martin tapped the list gently with his fingers.

"Missing? What do you mean?"

"Harry, listen!" Martin looked up, his expression as eager as a terrier's. "I want you to put yourself in Andy Mason's shoes for a moment. You're in a tight corner — or you think you are — and you suddenly decide to make a dash for it."

"Well?"

"What would be the first thing you'd think of — the first thing you'd want to take with you?"

"My wife."

"Andy Mason hadn't a wife!"

"I don't know. I can't imagine . . ."

"Think!"

"Well, I suppose I'd . . ." Kennedy scratched his head and frowned over the list. Then his face lit up as the penny dropped. "My passport!"

"Right! But it's not mentioned. It wasn't in his pockets, it wasn't in his baggage, and it wasn't in the car!"

"You're right . . . That's damn funny — I hardly think he'd forget his passport."

"He didn't!"

"What do you mean?" The Sergeant was still some way behind his superior.

"I don't believe it was Andy Mason that was killed!"

"What?"

"You said yourself his face was so badly disfigured that he was hardly recognisable," Martin pointed out, coming round the edge of the desk.

"Yes, but we saw him leave The Grapevine! Two of our chaps followed him."

"And then lost him! Do you know what I think? I think he had a body in that car . . ."

Kennedy laughed. "You've got to be joking."

"Yes, and that's why he went beserk and drove like a madman!"

"You mean he faked the crash and set fire to the car himself?" "Yes. Don't you see?"

"But, who?" Kennedy shook his head, wondering whether his own brains had gone soft or the Inspector had gone off his nut. "Whose body was it? If it wasn't Andy Mason — who the hell was it?"

"I'll give you one guess!" Martin said, grinning. "Just one guess, Harry, my boy!"

Kennedy bunched his fist and thumped the table. "Pike!"

The Inspector had already picked up the telephone and was starting to dial a number.

Andy Mason slackened speed and braked sharply. The sign at the end of the minor road on the right bore an arrow and the words Fleetway Flying Club. He swung the rented Vauxhall Cavalier across the front of an oncoming lorry and entered the lane. A glance at his watch told him that it was a quarter past ten.

Andy had stayed near the burning Ford Capri for long enough to be confident that the flames had made Pike's body unrecognisable until a proper post mortem was held. That would take half a day at any rate, ample time for him to put his hastily devised escape plan into operation. He walked the six miles into Reading, resisting the temptation to thumb a lift. He did not want any driver to get a good enough look at him to be able to describe him to the police.

He turned into the first hotel he found open, told a story about a seized engine and borrowed an electric razor before sitting down to an early breakfast. He had to wait till nine before he could telephone the car-hire people and it was a further forty-five minutes before the car was delivered and all the documents filled out. The flying club was twenty miles away, but he covered the distance in half an hour, despite the morning rush-hour traffic round Reading.

The airfield had been a war-time United States airforce base. The Fleetway Flying Club had renovated some of the buildings to form a small office block and club rooms. The only new building was a low brick construction, whose upper storey was glassed on all sides. It hardly seemed imposing enough to merit the title Control Tower.

It was a brilliant sunny morning as Andy cruised slowly up the lane, turned in through the gate and followed the old taxiing track round to the club buildings. Half a dozen light aircraft were parked near the one hangar which was still in use. He could see a mechanic in white overalls working on the engine of a blue Piper. There were only two cars parked outside the buildings. The club's activities were mostly confined to the weekends and a few summer evenings.

Bill Fenton, a small but broad man with a close beard, was in the office when Andy pushed the door open. He was wearing his most affable smile.

"Good morning, Bill. You've got everything fixed up for me?"

"Just about. The Piper suit you? I know you've done quite a few hours on it."

"That's fine. Is it ready to roll right away?"

"Will be before long. Fred's checking out the fuel system. It's been giving a bit of trouble lately. How much fuel are you going to need?"

"Better give me a full tank. I want to get in as many hours as I can. I haven't been doing nearly enough flying lately. Look, I'll go and get kitted up. Give Fred a shout to hurry it up."

Andy went through to the locker room and made sure it was empty before he unlocked his own steel cupboard. From the top shelf he took the wad of traveller's cheques which he'd been keeping there for some time now — just in case. He put them in his pocket, pulled on the set of light overalls and picked up the helmet with its built-in head-set and microphone. The walls were thin enough for him to hear the telephone ringing in the office and Bill Fenton's monosyllabic replies. The conversation was a short one. Bill had put down the receiver and was back at his desk when Andy came in, swinging his flying helmet by the strap. The leads, which would plug into the sockets in the aircraft, trailed to the ground.

Andy sat down on one of the club seats and began to flick through a flying magazine. After five minutes he threw it down and walked over to Bill's desk.

"Fred knows I'm here, I suppose?"

"Yes, I told him," Bill answered without looking up.

Andy frowned at the top of Bill's head. There was something different about Bill's manner. He was reluctant to look Andy in the face any more. A nerve began to twitch in the side of Andy's face.

"I think I'll stroll out and hurry him up," he said casually and turned to the door.

Bill's chair went back so fast that it fell over.

"I wouldn't do that, Andy. Anyway you've got to have clearance from the control tower before you can take off. We've just had a message from the RAF that they're doing some low flying in this area."

Bill had actually gone so far as to stand between him and the door.

Andy said, quietly: "They've never done that before. The RAF never practise low flying over these populated areas."

"Well — er. You know how it is. We have to play ball with them."

Andy's eyes went past Bill, through the window which looked across the airfield towards the approach road. Through the gaps in the hedge bordering the lane he had caught sight of a blue roof-light intermittently flashing.

"That call wasn't from the RAF, was it, Bill?"

Bill Fenton thought he knew Andy Mason, but the face which looked at him now was very different from the usual friendly pose.

"No, Andy. It wasn't. It was the police and my advice to you is wait here quite quietly till they come. I'm sorry, but you're not going out through this door."

"No?" said Andy. He put his hand through the slit in the overalls and withdrew the automatic from his pocket. Bill Fenton instantly interpreted the move and tried to rush him. Andy's bullet hit him in the stomach. He clutched himself with both hands and rolled to the floor.

Andy quickly pocketed the automatic and went out through the door. As he emerged he heard it clearly, the sound of a police siren warning anyone in the lane that a patrol car was coming along it fast. Andy deliberately slowed his pace as he walked over to the Piper. Fred was wiping his hands on a piece of cotton waste.

"She ready, Fred?"

"Just about. All I have to do is start her up again and test the fuel flow. What was that bang?"

"Some car back-firing," Andy said easily. "You needn't test her. I can do that when I'm going through my checks."

"You know that's against regs, Mr. Mason," the mechanic

said with dogged righteousness. His head jerked round as once again the sound of a siren floated across the airfield. "Cor, what's that? Sounded like a police siren. Blimey, there's two of them!"

The police cars were now moving fast along the last stretch of the lane. In a matter of seconds they would arrive on the airfield proper. Andy reached into his pocket and again gripped the automatic. The mechanic turned in time to see his hand come out with the weapon in it. Fred had been in the RAF in Aden and had learned to think and react quickly. It was almost a reflex action to throw the heavy spanner he was holding in his hand. It struck Andy hard on the right shoulder. An agonising pain shot down his arm, causing him to drop the gun.

As he stooped to recover it, Fred leaped on him. The two men rolled on the ground, the mechanic wincing as the hard shape of the gun dug into his back. Andy's eyes were crazy now and his strength astonished Fred, who concentrated all his efforts on staying as he was, masking the gun. But Andy had him by the wrist and was twisting the spanner out of his grasp. Fred shouted with pain, released his grip and let the spanner fall. Andy picked it up and hit Fred a vicious blow on the temple. His head jerked back and he lay limp.

Andy struggled to his feet. The two police cars had entered the airfield and were racing towards the office buildings. They had not sported him yet. The operator in the control tower had abandoned his post and was running towards the police cars, waving his arms. Someone else had come out of the club buildings.

Abandoning the helmet which had fallen on the ground Andy raced to the aircraft and climbed aboard. The engine was warm and started immediately. Ignoring the mandatory checklist Andy increased revs and began to taxi to the end of the take-off runway.

On the ground behind him the mechanic shook his head and opened his eyes. He rolled sideways clear of the gun. He picked it up and, holding it with both hands, fired a shot at the receding Piper. The metallic clang told him that he had found a mark. Petrol started pouring from the hole in the fuel tank.

Martin was in the passenger's seat of the leading police car, and Kennedy was in the back with the driver's colleague. They'd covered the forty miles from Guildfleet in less than three quarters of an hour, only to be held up in the last mile by a herd of cows.

The driver needed no instructions to drive towards the control tower operator, who was running across the grass, waving his arms. Martin lowered the window as the car skidded to a halt beside him.

"What's happening?"

"I don't know. It's one of our members. He must have gone mad. He's knocked out the mechanic. He can't take off! I haven't given him clearance yet."

"He'll take off," Martin said, grimly. He stepped out of the car and signalled the second vehicle towards him. "See that aircraft on the runway? You've got to head him off before he gets airborne."

The driver nodded and his wheels spun as he accelerated away. The Piper had just turned and was lining up for take off.

Kennedy dismounted and stood beside the Inspector.

"We just missed him. If it hadn't been for those blasted cows we'd have got him."

An ambulance, one of the special bodies mounted on the Citroen chassis, had emerged from behind the club buildings and was racing towards the prone form of the mechanic. The second police car, raising a cloud of dust, was travelling ever faster on a line that would converge with the Piper, which had now started its take-off run.

There was nothing Martin and Kennedy could do now except watch the race.

"What's that spray coming out the back?" Kennedy pointed excitedly. "Can he be losing petrol?"

"Don't know," Martin replied tersely, his eyes switching from the car to the aircraft and back again.

At first it seemed that the police car would easily head the taxiing aircraft off, but as the Piper gathered speed the Volvo began to lose ground. The two machines were racing now on almost parallel courses. Realising that he was losing the race, the police driver did a crazy but courageous thing. He locked hard over and, with spinning wheels, headed in right on the path of the Piper. Andy Mason was now committed to take off. He could not have stopped even if he had wanted to, and he obviously could not alter course till he was airborne. The police car slid to a halt right in his path. For an instant the crash seemed inevitable.

Three hundred yards away Martin half closed his eyes and muttered: "My God!"

Then he saw the nose of the aircraft lift. It rose sharply, its landing wheels missing the roof of the car by inches.

"That was nearly a posthumous police medal," he commented.

The officers in the distant car had now piled out and were staring in frustration at the receding aircraft as it gained height over the trees surrounding the airfield. The stream of liquid was still spewing from the holed petrol tank. The ambulance men had placed the mechanic on a stretcher and were loading it into the ambulance. The dozen or so people employed on the field had come out of their buildings and were staring at the sky, shading their eyes as they watched the fading silhouette of the Piper.

"We'd better alert all airfields in the vicinity," Kennedy suggested. "He won't get far with a leaking petrol tank."

Martin put a hand on his arm to stop him. The buzz of the Piper had ceased. They could clearly hear a series of crackles as the pumps sucked on an empty tank. The little machine had lost height rapidly and was already below the line of the trees.

Ten seconds later the sound of a deep explosion reached their ears. It was another half minute before the smoke column rose into view. A black, oily cloud was spreading across the sky in almost leisurely fashion.

Kennedy looked at Martin.

"I don't suppose there's much left of him," Martin said, "but we'd better go and pick up the pieces, Harry. I wonder if the Fleetway Flying Club runs to a helicopter?"

It was all over by lunchtime, bar the full report which would have to be written. By the time the fire-tender had got near enough to put out the fire the body of Andy Mason was in an even more terrible state than Pike's.

Martin tried to banish the memory from his mind when he picked up Sue, but she noticed his silence as they drove out to the cottage.

At last she dared to ask him: "How did it go? Were you able to arrest him?"

"The case is finished, Sue. I'd rather not talk about it any more for the moment."

He said nothing for a few minutes and gradually the tension went out of him.

"I've been thinking about your idea for redecorating the house and putting up new curtains. I'm all for it. But you've got to choose the colours. I'm no good at that sort of thing."

Her fingers were at the back of his head, soothing and caressing. Disregarding the police driving code, he put a hand on her thigh.

"You know the first thing I'm going to do when we get to the cottage?"

"Carry me over the threshold?" she suggested, smiling.

"No. That comes later. First I'm going to take down that damned 'For Sale' notice."

Lightning Source UK Ltd.
Milton Keynes UK
UKOW04f0152060315

247373UK00002B/179/P